THE HEIR
& THE SPARE

Also by Harper L. Woods

COVEN OF BONES
The Coven
The Cursed
The Damned

OF FLESH & BONE
What Lies Beyond the Veil
What Hunts Inside the Shadows
What Lurks Between the Fates
What Sleeps Within the Cove

THE HEIR & THE SPARE

HARPER L. WOODS

BRAMBLE

Tor Publishing Group
New York

This is a work of fiction. All of the characters, organizations, and events portrayed in this novel are either products of the author's imagination or are used fictitiously.

THE HEIR & THE SPARE

Copyright © 2026 by Harper L. Woods

All rights reserved.

A Bramble Book
Published by Tom Doherty Associates / Tor Publishing Group
120 Broadway
New York, NY 10271

www.torpublishinggroup.com

Bramble™ is a trademark of Macmillan Publishing Group, LLC.

EU Representative: Macmillan Publishers Ireland Ltd, 1st Floor, The Liffey Trust Centre, 117–126 Sheriff Street Upper, Dublin 1, DO1 YC43

The Library of Congress Cataloging-in-Publication Data is available upon request.

ISBN 978-1-250-42385-6 (hardcover)
ISBN 978-1-250-42386-3 (ebook)

The publisher of this book does not authorize the use or reproduction of any part of this book in any manner for the purpose of training artificial intelligence technologies or systems. The publisher of this book expressly reserves this book from the Text and Data Mining exception in accordance with Article 4(3) of the European Union Digital Single Market Directive 2019/790.

Our books may be purchased in bulk for specialty retail/wholesale, literacy, corporate/premium, educational, and subscription box use. Please contact MacmillanSpecialMarkets@macmillan.com.

First Edition: 2026

Printed in the United States of America

10 9 8 7 6 5 4 3 2 1

For the ones who cannot be contained

Author's Note

The Heir & the Spare is set within the Of Flesh & Bone world. For the best reading experience, it should be read after book four of the series, *What Sleeps Within the Cove*, to fully understand the circumstances and characters that have led Fallon and Etan to where they will be in book five, *What Roams Beneath the Stars*. As such, *The Heir & the Spare* will contain major spoilers for the first three books in the series.

The Of Flesh & Bone series is set in a medieval-style world where human women are subservient to their male counterparts. The world is a dark, dangerous place for women, particularly those who do not conform to societal standards and the purity culture that determines how they live.

The Fae realm of Alfheimr is even darker, and the violence in this world gets darker and more graphic with each book. There is murder, torture, and elements of assault.

As such, some elements may be triggering to certain readers. Please proceed with caution.

- Religious purity culture
- Verbal and physical abuse (NOT by the male lead)
- References to grooming behavior and assault of a minor by an authority figure (NOT by the male lead)
- References to past physical and sexual abuse
- Ritualistic sacrifices
- Suicide
- Suicidal thoughts and ideation
- Graphic death, violence, and torture
- Attempted sexual assault (NOT by the male lead)
- Graphic sexual content
- Flesh-eating creatures

GLOSSARY

Alfheimr: The Fae realm.

Calfalls: The Ruined City that was once a tribute to the God of the Dead before he destroyed it in the war between the Fae and humans.

High Priest/Priestess: The top Priest and Priestess, who profess to commune with The Father and The Mother and pass along their messages.

Ineburn City: The capital of the human realm, a gleaming city of gold.

Mistfell: The village at the edge of the Veil, where it is closest to Alfheimr. Serves as the access point between realms when the Veil does not block passage.

Mist Guard: A separate army with the sole purpose of protecting the Veil from harm and fighting the Fae should it ever fall.

New Gods: The Father and The Mother. Worshiped by humans after they discovered the truth that the Old Gods were truly Fae. The Father and The Mother make the choice of whether a soul goes to Valhalla, Folkvangr, or Helheim after the true death at the end of the thirteen-life cycle.

Nothrek: The human realm.

Old Gods: The Old Gods are the most powerful of the Fae race known as the Sidhe. Most commonly, these are the offspring of the Primordials.

Priest/Priestess: The men and women who lead the Temple in service of the New Gods and their wishes (The Father and The Mother).

Primordials: The first beings in all of creation. They do not have a human form by nature, though they can choose to take one for various reasons and are simply the personification of what they represent.

Resistance, The: A secret society living in the tunnels of the Hollow Mountains (as well as elsewhere in Nothrek) that resist the rules of the Kingdom and live their lives as they please. They also resist the Fae and offer protection to the Fae Marked and other refugees fleeing the Royal or Mist Guard.

Royal Guard: The army that works on behalf of the King of Nothrek, ensuring that the Kingdom remains peaceful and compliant with his wishes.

Sidhe: The humanlike Fae who are *not* of the first generations and are less powerful than the Old Gods. Their magic exists, but is far more limited than their older counterparts.

Veil: The magical boundary that separates the human realm of Nothrek from the Fae realm of Alfheimr.

Viniculum: The physical symbol of the Fae Marked. Swirling ink in the color of the Fae's home court extending from the hand to the shoulder/chest.

Wild Hunt: The group of ghostlike Fae from the Shadow Court that are tasked with tracking down the Fae Marked to return them to their mates in Alfheimr, as well as hunting any who may be deemed enemies to the Fae.

Witches: Immortal beings with powers relating to the elements and celestial bodies; i.e., the Shadow Witches, Lunar Witches, Natural Witches, Water Witches, etc.

HIERARCHY OF THE GODS & FAE PRIMORDIALS

Khaos: Primordial of the Void that existed before all creation
Ilta: Primordial of the Night
Edrus: Primordial of Darkness
Zain: Primordial of the Sky
Diell: Primordial of the Day
Ubel: Primordial responsible for the prison of Tartarus
Bryn: Primordial of Nature
Oshun: Primordial of the Sea
Gerwyn: Primordial of Love
Aerwyna: Primordial of the Sea Creatures
Tempest: Primordial of Storms
Peri: Primordial of the Mountains
Sauda: Primordial of Poisons
Anke: Primordial of Compulsion
Marat: Primordial of Light
Eylam: Primordial of Time
The Fates: Primordial of Destiny
Ahimoth: Primordial of Impending Doom

OLD GODS OF NOTE

Aderyn: Goddess of the Harvest and Queen of the Autumn Court
Alastor: King of the Winter Court and husband to Twyla before his death
Caldris: God of the Dead
Jonab: God of Changing Seasons. Killed during the First Fae War.
Kahlo: God of Beasts and King of the Autumn Court
Mab: Queen of the Shadow Court. Known mainly as the Queen of Air and Darkness. Sister to Rheaghan (King of the Summer Court).
Rheaghan: God of the Sun and King of the Summer Court. Rightful King of the Seelie.
Sephtis: God of the Underworld and King of the Shadow Court
Shena: Goddess of Plant Life and Queen of the Spring Court
Tiam: God of Youth and King of the Spring Court
Twyla: Goddess of the Moon and Queen of the Winter Court. Rightful Queen of the Unseelie.
The Wild Hunt
Sidhe

THE HEIR & THE SPARE

One

ETAN

It was never easy.

I couldn't imagine it was for any of us who were trapped within the confines of Mab's court. I could only be grateful that she'd determined my greatest use to her was remaining in the Summer Court I called home. So many of us weren't so lucky. So many of us were never gifted the opportunity to escape her violence and madness. Whereas I had only been present in Tar Mesa for a few days, others had been trapped here for decades—centuries even.

I had lost count of the number of Fae I had watched Mab torture over my centuries of life as Rheaghan's second-in-command. At some point, I'd become a hollow shell of the man I'd once been, strictly out of the need to survive. There was nothing I stood to gain by interfering in her games—nothing but the call of the final death and the freedom that would finally come with it.

There were people who counted on me, and I'd told myself that my silence served the greater good. My willingness to make hard choices meant that the majority of my court could stay healthy and happy and as far away from Mab as possible.

So why did the sight of Mab torturing her own daughter nearly drive me to do the one thing I had never risked?

The Princess Maeve was a mess of bloody ribbons, her flesh torn open by Mab's shadows. She'd been so determined to find out what sort of magic her daughter had at her disposal that it was clear any hopes we'd had for their reunification had been entirely foolish. There had been the smallest glimmer of hope that the love for her daughter would have been enough to peek through the madness and tame the worst of Mab's impulses, but it seemed Maeve was just as subject to them as the rest of us.

For her part, Maeve had never revealed what her mother wanted. The Princess was already a beautiful woman, with fair skin as if it had never seen the light and hair as dark as night. She was striking, an unusual but ethereal beauty, with wide-set hazel eyes and full, pouty lips. She'd braided her hair away from her face on one side in tight twists, revealing a deep scar that slashed from her forehead to her cheek and bisected her eyebrow.

She looked the part of the warrior, and the defiance and determination she'd shown in refusing to display her magic to Mab only reinforced that—only made her all the more striking to behold. Her strength made me want to protect her, a completely unrealistic drive that made no sense for the woman I had never even spoken to. Something in her called to me—convinced me that she was used to standing alone.

Nobody should have to be alone.

I'd refrained from interfering by clenching my hands into fists at my sides—reminding myself that Rheaghan needed me and the cover my alleged allegiance to Mab provided.

She could barely walk by the time Mab was finished with her, attempting to draw out any source of magic and willing to use any means necessary to do so. The Queen of Air and Darkness's desperation to have a daughter who could be *used* was tangible in the air, her disappointment when nothing came driving her to the point of rage. It was as if the sudden presence of her child actively worsened her madness instead of alleviating it.

It did not help that Caldris's mate had proven to be far more interesting than Mab had anticipated when she'd first taken her days prior, displaying magic that should have been so far beyond her reach as a human mate. I'd heard whispers over the years I'd spent spying on all of Mab's faithful on Rheaghan's behalf, the hushed murmurs spoken in shadows in an attempt to keep Mab from knowing of the second child that had been taken from Alfheimr and tucked out of reach in Nothrek with the Veil to protect her.

I couldn't say for sure if those whispers had ever reached her ears or if she remained entirely oblivious. The information wasn't typically filed away as something critical to run to her with, given the rumorous nature of it at its core. To present information to Mab that proved to be false would draw unwanted attention to the messenger, and being caught in Mab's crosshairs was not a position many wanted to risk. Many chose to take the odds of her never discovering their knowledge of the rumor if it came to fruition, but there was no winning in any situation where Mab was involved.

There were very few of us who thought we could play games with her and come out alive on the other side. In spite of all of Rheaghan's warnings, I couldn't help but enjoy the calm, manipulative whispers that I murmured in the Queen's ears to try to gain luxuries and freedoms for the people of the Summer Court that they might not have had if it hadn't been for my interference.

She was just as likely to punish them in her attempt to harm her brother as she was to reward them for their loyalty to her.

Rheaghan cleared his throat, forcing me to snap out of the trance where I'd been staring at the Princess and lost in thought. "Don't even think about it," the King of the Summer Court said, and I turned my stare away from the breathtaking woman, who I realized, with a shock of discomfort, was his niece.

Oops.

I laughed, brushing my hand over the back of my neck as I searched for the words to argue that what she did, as a fully grown woman, was none of his business. Even for the Fae, who were more open in the lines of taboo and what relationships were forbidden, ogling your best friend's niece was a little suspect.

"I'm not sure what you're talking about," I said, shrugging my shoulders to feign casualness about the situation. Even if he didn't want to think about it, which would have been even stranger than normal considering he had never met the woman before, he would find himself in the uncomfortable position of men admiring her.

"Don't give me that bullshit. Getting involved with Mab's daughter would be the very definition of stupid. That's not even touching on the awkwardness of me being obligated to beat your ass if you touch my niece," Rheaghan said, arching a brow at me.

"Maybe, but I've never claimed to be smart," I said, grinning through the words as the King of the Summer Court hung his head forward and pinched the bridge of his nose in exasperation.

"I would like to see you survive long enough to return home at the end of the Tithe. Call me selfish," he snarked, but he knew as well as I did that the damage was done. Like so many others of our kind, particularly those from the Summer Court, where blood ran as hot as the desert plains that surrounded our seaside homes, I was not easily deterred from something after I set my mind to it, and I wanted to *know* Princess Maeve.

Intimately.

The Princess stumbled her way down the aisle of the throne room, making her way to the doors at the back as Devorin trailed behind her. The gown they'd put her in before returning her to the throne room was too long in the back, trailing behind her in a sea of black that matched her hair.

Mab's propensity for pomp and circumstance meant that I was used to seeing women in the finery that she demanded, gowns being the most common attire in Tar Mesa, but there was something about the way Maeve moved that signaled a discomfort with the garment.

Wherever she'd lived, whatever life she'd come from, she wasn't used to the feeling of a dress playing around at her ankles or the heeled shoes they'd put on her feet.

I stepped forward from the shadows when she tripped on the dress, catching her by her forearms and keeping her from falling. Her blood slicked my hands, coating my palms in the places where Mab had bled her in an attempt to draw out her magic.

She paused for a moment, letting me support her in what I knew was the first deep breath she'd taken since entering that throne room and facing down the woman she had probably come to dread meeting, despite their blood relation. When she finally raised her chin to meet my stare, something hard glittered behind her hazel eyes that reminded me of molten steel, of heat and flame that burned so hot it could destroy all that remained of the world that had been ravaged by Mab's cruelty.

I held her still, my mouth dropping open as we lingered for a moment, tuning out the noise and commotion of Mab's court around us.

"Princess Maeve," I said finally, bowing my head forward in the sign of respect her mother would expect from me. Her jaw hardened to match her eyes, her nostrils flaring with annoyance.

"My. Name. Is. Fallon," she snapped, the ire in her voice tipping the corners of my mouth up into a smile. Many would have broken under Mab's torturous hands, would have caved and given her anything she wanted, but this woman clung to all traces of her identity and rebelled against the control the Queen of Air and Darkness would try to exert over her life.

Immediately, I knew Rheaghan and I needed to do whatever it took to free her from Tar Mesa and the direct influence of Mab in her daily life as quickly as possible. That rebellious spirit would be her downfall if she didn't find the balance to prove herself useful to Mab. If Rheaghan and I left her here, we'd be condemning her to death.

It may not happen the next day, or even the week after, but eventually that spirit would be crushed beneath Mab's fist until death became a mercy. Rheaghan and Mab's mother had practically raised me. Her memory deserved better than watching her lineage die.

"Fallon," I whispered as I turned to nod at her mother where she watched our interaction, offering Fallon my arm as I took my place beside her. She accepted it, even though it seemed like she may not, allowing me to lend my support as she gathered her dress in her free hand and tugged, tearing the fabric at her knees and tossing it to the side with a glare for Mab.

I withheld my chuckle and my grin, impressing both Rheaghan and myself when he wasn't able to stop the hoarse snort that he attempted to cover with his hand. She let me guide her forward, putting distance between us and the Queen, who would undoubtedly be angry at the torn gown.

As if it weren't already ruined by her daughter's blood.

Malachi, the sadistic bastard, took her other arm the moment we were out of Mab's sight, guiding her away from me and toward the hall that would lead to the stairs and up to the rooms Mab had chosen for her. I watched her go as Rheaghan came up beside me, his hands stuffed into his trouser pockets.

She took a few steps with Malachi's assistance, his attention to her struggle reassuring me ever so slightly. He would keep her as safe as he could, from any threat outside of his precious Queen, because Fallon was the lost Princess that all of Tar Mesa had wished would return for the centuries since she'd disappeared in the night. But I didn't know that the worship they had for her would last, now that we'd been faced with the reality that Mab cared very little for the woman we'd all hoped would tame her by giving her someone to love.

She stopped halfway up the steps, turning to meet my stare over her shoulder for the briefest of moments. It was all I needed to reassure me that my intentions for her would be met with returned interest.

She felt that pull, that inexplicable attraction that had consumed me from the moment I saw her. It made no sense given the reality that I had yet to feel the pull of my mate, even after the fall of the Veil.

Condemned to live alone for centuries, I was tired of waiting endlessly for a woman who may never come.

For one who might have died her final, true death before the Veil came down, leaving me to rot in madness for the rest of eternity until Rheaghan or someone else I loved had to put me down as a mercy.

No, I was done fucking waiting for my mate.

I'd claim a wife instead.

Two

FALLON

I hissed through my teeth, refusing to give her the benefit of hearing my screams. She sat back on her throne with a bored expression as she flicked her wrist, twining her shadows and darkness in a serpentine pattern. They wrapped around my forearm, squeezing tighter and tighter until the pressure built to an apex that felt like it might tear something out of me.

I couldn't breathe as that strange pressure rose in my chest in time with the tightening shadows on my arm. Blood welled beneath them as they writhed and dug deeper, sawing their way through my flesh until white-hot pain spread through me and they wrapped around the bone.

My skin felt too warm as it spread through my blood. Mab leaned forward as I raised my eyes to glare at her, gritting my teeth through the pain that was so much worse than anything I could remember.

Even the wound on my face hadn't compared to *this*, even if solely because I'd been knocked unconscious for the worst of it before Imelda could get to me.

She tapped the fingers of her free hand against the arm of her throne before she stood, curling her fingers and twisting her wrist suddenly so the palm that had faced the floor now faced the ceiling.

The snap of my bones tore a grunt from my mouth, the sound louder than I'd intended. I refused to look down at my arm, too aware of the way it felt *wrong*. I'd never done well with the sight of broken bones and the unnatural angles that went along with them.

Blood I could handle, but something about broken bones made me lightheaded.

Mab grimaced as she descended the steps of the dais, the otherwise silent throne room feeling too still as she raised her free hand and struck my shoulder with her shadow. It sank deep into the skin, using the penetration to force my shoulders back and hold me still as she approached.

She stopped before me, leaning lower until she was in my face where I knelt at the base of the dais. She paused long enough to observe the small crowd behind us, her loyal followers who had been welcomed to witness my torture. Even with all the hours that had passed the day before without success, she still believed I would break.

"Release it," she ordered, speaking the words under her breath. She kept them a soft hush between us, so that it was only for the two of us to know, and I didn't understand how she sensed the magic clinging to my heart and soul, but she did.

She *knew* it was there. Knew it was within me and I just refused to let it out.

My rage burned hotter, feeling like the fires of a thousand suns as my lips peeled back into a feral snarl. I spit at her, the red stain of blood striking her cheek as someone behind me gasped. "I hope whoever kills you tears you limb from limb," I said, wincing when she wrapped her hand around the front of my throat and lifted me to my feet.

The shadows she'd used to torture me didn't move with me, tearing through my skin anew. The ones wrapped around my forearm pulled down, yanking at the joints and stretching muscles beyond what was natural. The shadow that pierced my shoulder tore through my flesh as I rose, sliding down to cut a path through my chest and the side of my breast.

"Should we find out if you can survive that very thing?" Mab asked, tugging at my arm until I felt a distinctive popping sensation.

"That's enough," Rheaghan said, stepping forward until he stood beside me. Magic rose on his hands with the brightness of day, chasing away the shadows of his sister's magic. I'd only met him once, at the dinner Mab had hosted after the royals from the other courts arrived for the Tithe a few days prior.

The shadows shrank back from his light, and Mab didn't bother to fight him as he drew me into his side and supported the weight that felt too heavy for me to carry alone. Another figure took the side of my broken arm, carefully avoiding touching it but offering a supportive hand at my back. I turned to find the man from the day before standing there, his warm eyes searching my face as if he could judge my level of pain.

"I think we should all take a step back for the night. Perhaps we can acknowledge that this has gone too far," he said, his voice quiet. I expected Mab to bristle at the condemning words that insinuated she had been in the wrong for torturing me, but instead she only grimaced and reached out a hand to take the stranger's in hers.

"I was only having some fun," she said, her lips twisting into a pout that felt far too childlike.

"Fallon is your daughter, my Queen. Not one of your playthings. Choose another to entertain your more . . . vicious urges," he said, a one-sided smile curving his lips.

"Oh, very well." Mab laughed, a childish giggle spilling free as she turned away from me with glee. The two men took advantage of her distraction to guide me out of the throne room and help me to my room, leaving me with a singular question pounding in my brain.

Who the fuck was he, and why did Mab listen to him?

I stripped the remaining fabric from the dress off my shoulders after they left me at my room, ignoring the Sidhe woman who attempted to help me out of it as I shredded it in the process. My throat burned with the threat of tears I would never let fall with an audience, the emotion of the night threatening to consume me.

Watching Mab torture Estrella had been bad enough. Watching her toy with her and threaten to whip her in a way that I just knew would leave permanent scars had threatened to tear me in two, and the amount of pride I felt when Estrella stood her ground and shocked Mab was immense.

Until Mab had sent her to the dungeon and turned her attention to me, focusing all that anger on my skin. She hadn't relented once since, determined to draw some semblance of power from me.

This was my mother. This was the woman who had brought me into the world and created my very soul. If this was what she was capable of doing to her own flesh and blood, then I shuddered to think of what she would do to strangers, or those she considered her enemies. Imelda had never kept secrets from me. While she hadn't known whether it was me or Estrella who was Mab's daughter, she'd told me stories of Mab's cruelty—knowing it would likely one day affect me either way.

The knock that came at the door had me snatching the blanket from the bed and wrapping it around my chest. Nudity did not bother me in the slightest under normal circumstances, but the very thought of being naked before someone who came to do me harm was a different concept altogether.

"Fallon," Imelda's soft voice called from the other side, making everything within me deflate and relax. I nodded to the Sidhe woman, Pax, and she returned the gesture, hurrying to the door in silence. She waved Imelda inside, quickly closing the door to shut me away from anyone who may be lingering in the hall. Even in those brief moments of looking through the cracked door, I hadn't missed the guard stationed outside it.

Meant to protect me, he'd said.

Meant to imprison me sounded more accurate.

Imelda closed the distance between us in a rush, cupping my cheeks in her hand and staring down at me as she weighed the extent of my injuries. "Leave us," she snapped to the Sidhe woman, but she smiled softly as if it would take away the sting. "Please," she added, the word soothing the uncomfortable lines on the woman's face.

Pax nodded, clasping her hands in front of her. "I've already prepared a hot bath for you, Princess. I'll be in the adjoining room if you need anything," she said, making her way to the door on the side wall. The bedroom within was tiny compared to the opulence of mine, a mere bed and single cabinet for her belongings. She brought one of the candles with her to illuminate the space where she disappeared, and I couldn't help the surge of guilt I felt that she was relegated to what was practically a closet.

Tomorrow, I would care. Tomorrow, I would tell her she was welcome to stay with me in my room. Today, I just needed the space to be with Imelda in private.

I needed the space to break, and finally having the one constant in my life at my side was the best way to do that.

The moment Pax closed the door, Imelda tugged me into her embrace. Her skin was familiar where it touched mine, cool and comforting in a way that reminded me of the snow I now knew the feel of. A chill ran through me, but I couldn't seem to tear myself away as she ran her hands over the cuts Mab had left behind. They'd already begun to heal, the odd nature of the Fae making itself known now that my entire being had shifted.

There hadn't been time to even consider the implications of that. I'd still been reeling from it on the snow when Mab and her men had stormed in and taken Estrella and me to Tar Mesa. My hands involuntarily moved to my ears, trembling as they touched the pointed tips.

The people I'd lived with, the family I had known for as long as I could remember, hated everything to do with the Fae. They hated *me*.

A strangled sob caught in my throat, but I wouldn't let that unfamiliar sting of tears become anything real. I would not cry for the things I couldn't control. Instead, I let the chill of Imelda's skin soothe my wounds, acting like ice and numbing them as she held me.

Eventually, she separated from me long enough to drop the bag she always kept strapped across her body to the dining table, hauling open the flap and pulling out herbs and vials and all manner of things.

"Sit," she ordered, using her foot to push out one of the chairs. I did as I was told and lowered myself into it, hating that there was no point in arguing with her. I would heal in time, and it wouldn't even be an extended period. She grabbed a clean cloth from her bag, then opened a vial of water I knew she'd placed outside under the last full moon and poured some of the liquid onto it. She used that to wipe the dried and fresh blood from my arms, giving her a better look at what remained of my injuries as she tended to me.

"I'll be okay, Imelda," I said, stilling her hands when she set to work frantically tearing herbs from their stems and putting them into the mortar that would have weighed down any normal person with an average bag. She added a drop of oil I'd watched her press from the stem of a rosemary plant from the hidden gardens we tended to in the summer months.

"I know you will," she said, her voice laced with steady determination. She added a drop of full-moon water to the mortar, grinding the herbs into the oil and liquid with her pestle. Her entire arm moved with the motion of it, determined to grind it into a paste I'd seen her use to heal the humans and prevent infection.

I knew the cost that came with her healing, understood it after seeing it for myself countless times. It wasn't necessary here.

"Imelda," I snapped, finally getting her to look at me. "No magic."

Her head rocked back, her mouth parting in shock as she stared at the thin lines covering my arms. Already the bleeding had slowed to a stop, the skin working to knit itself back together as we watched it. Imelda dropped her hands at her sides, the reality of what I was striking her as hard as it had me.

How many times had she healed my injuries? Taken the knees I scraped as a child upon herself and left me blemish-free?

The scar that remained on my face was a testament of her skill, the wound left by the cave beast when I'd been foolish as a teen and thought myself skilled enough to wander the tunnels on my own. It had gouged deep enough that I would have died without her magic, that the claw that had shredded my eye would have taken my sight at the very least.

She'd managed to sew my flesh together, to save my eye entirely, before her magic ran out, the Veil separating her from the full extent of it.

Imelda had slept for a week after, my worry forcing me to sit vigil at her bedside with the knowledge that it had been my fault, my own stupidity, that had taken nearly everything from her.

I'd never left the tunnels we called home again. Not until Caldris and Estrella came to collect me.

"But—" Imelda began to argue. I knew her well enough to understand that she had long since come to associate her worth with her ability to heal those around her, never once understanding that sometimes it was okay for her to weigh her own well-being against that of others. The way she fidgeted from one foot to the other was so unlike the calm and composed woman she presented to anyone else, leaning into the centuries of life she'd lived and what that meant.

Most of the humans in the tunnels had expected her to have all the answers, simply because she'd lived for so long. But her age didn't suddenly erase her heartaches or her trauma.

If anything, it gave her more time to accumulate them, and for those wounds to fester.

"I will heal these even faster than you would. There is no reason for you to waste your magic on the likes of me any longer. But—" I paused, hating the feel of the magic stirring in my veins. It had taken everything in me to shove it down while Mab cut my skin, and I knew it was only a matter of time before I gave in to the heat of it that pooled like lava in my gut. I'd felt the first faint stirring of it when I'd collapsed to the snow in Alfheimr, my skin warming as the magic touched me. That twitchy, warm feeling hadn't worsened over the days since.

But it was fucking exhausting.

"But?" Imelda asked, taking my hands and pulling me to stand. She guided me to the bath Pax had prepared, helping me shrug off the blanket that had become my makeshift robe. She tossed it back to the bed as I stepped into the bath, gritting my teeth through the heat as I lowered myself and the water stung my skin.

Imelda moved to her bag, grabbing herbs and the like for the water.

"But I need you to redo your wards on me," I said, watching as her brow furrowed as she approached the bath once more. The wards had once been intended to keep Mab from sensing me and using that pull to find me, but now—

"But you are Fae now. There is no reason to hide you from the Fae when you have already been found," she argued.

"I won't allow myself to be used. I will not allow myself to have magic if that is what she wants from me. I don't care what kind of magic flows through my veins, I need you to keep it quiet and hidden," I said, raising my chin high with defiance.

I would be everything Mab did not want me to be.

"She won't be pleased if you do not give her what she wants, *min nghaalon*," she said, the familiar term of affection warming something inside me. It felt like home, reminding me of all the times she gave me a lesson and needed me to focus on her teachings and all I wanted to do was run and play with the other children.

My heart.

"I believe it has become my life's mission to be her greatest disappointment. That is a challenge I think myself very capable of meeting," I said, smiling through the bitterness of the words.

Imelda didn't approve of my self-deprecating humor, frequently reminding me that I was meant for great things. But nothing could change the way a child felt when she wasn't allowed to do the things the other kids were, when she was so protected and treated as if she were fragile that she could not leave the sanctuary belowground.

Knowing why didn't lessen the sting.

I was far from greatness.

"She will hurt you again. Wanting to disappoint her out of spite is one thing, but at what cost to yourself? If you do not allow your magic to surface, then you can't ever learn to use it either. There may come a day where that puts you at a great disadvantage," Imelda warned, but as much as she wanted to protect me, I knew she would grant me this. When my desires aligned with what was best for all of Alfheimr and Nothrek combined, she could not argue against my decision.

She would grant me the right to make my own choices now, something that I'd been largely deprived of in my time with the Resistance.

"And I will heal all over again," I said, watching her sigh as she pulled the knife she kept strapped to her waist free from its scabbard. She drew it across her palm, making a shallow cut, before returning her knife to its rightful place.

She held out her palm, allowing her blood to drip into the water. The magic of the Lunar Coven immediately filled the water, the feeling of it on my skin reminding me of the nights we'd spent traveling. Resting on snow-covered ground by the fire, with the light of the moon shining down on me, the chill was unmistakable to my skin, which felt naturally hot since we'd come to the shores of Alfheimr.

"La solis ne lunat," Imelda said, her voice dropping lower as it moved into the trance of her magic. The moon inked on her forehead glowed in response to it, her lungs filling with air that seemed to surprise her.

It had been centuries since Imelda stepped foot in Alfheimr, since she too had the full extent of her magic at her fingertips. "Gods," I shuddered, the water of my bath filling with a hazy wisp. It moved through the water like smoke, like clouds spreading over the surface of the moon, as her eyes drifted closed and she plunged her hands into the water.

The sleeves of her dress were drenched immediately, but Imelda continued unbothered, as she wrapped her hands around my ankles and gripped me.

"Dion y dennaig kvinna, dolja a hud argi seallgowg, nes an kellar al-

wei namn," she said, cold spreading through my ankles and up my calves.

"*Le solid ne lunat, Dion y dennaig kvinna...*" she said, repeating her chant and pausing after each line. She continued three times, each iteration spreading her magic through my body until the force of it pulled me deeper into the bath.

I slid down the back of the tub, my face lingering above the surface of the water as I drew in deep breaths to prepare for what I knew would come.

This was so much more than what she'd done in the hot springs beneath the mountains.

Her magic was so much stronger than it ever had been there.

"*Nes an kellar alwei namn!*" she said, her voice dropping even lower on her final recital. Though her hands did not move, the strength of her magic pulled me under the surface of the water in the deep basin, plunging me down until water filled my lungs.

It burned with cold, searing me from the inside for only a brief moment before it released me. I sputtered as I came to the surface, coughing out water as I flung my dark hair out of my face and met Imelda's shocked gaze.

"That was..." I sputtered, coughing as I grinned at her. I felt nearly human, no press of heat in my veins and my skin feeling chilled in its absence.

Imelda swallowed. The strength of her spell had surprised her, too. "My power has grown since I left Alfheimr centuries ago," she said, shaking her head as she moved to the table and packed her bag.

"Isn't that a good thing?" I asked, pulling myself to stand as Imelda shook off her distraction and brought me a cloth to dry myself with.

"Perhaps," she said, but her gaze remained distant, lost in thought. "But it could also make me a target for the more ambitious of our coven—someone they see as a threat in the pursuit of power."

"One of these days, you will need to share the secrets of your coven with me," I said, smiling in an attempt to ease her obvious stress.

"One day, I will take you home to what remains of my coven, so they can see that all our sacrifice was worth every moment," she said, cupping my cheek briefly before backing away from me. She moved to the door without another word, leaving me to stare after her and wishing she would have stayed.

With a glance around the now empty room, I moved to the window at the edge and stared out over the sand-covered plains.

Her distance stung. I knew I could call her back easily and she would stay with me and offer me comfort. But Imelda had always had her secrets, a life before Nothrek that I knew nothing about.

I just hoped the ghosts of her past didn't interfere with her future now that she'd returned.

Three

ETAN

Rheaghan's warning was an echo in my mind as I paced in my room days later, feeling restless in my own skin with the need to take action. The memory of those searing hazel eyes was vivid in my mind and had haunted my every dream in the nights that had passed since I'd last seen her. I'd done everything I could to avoid her, thinking distance would be enough to make me forget the way her skin felt on mine.

The way her blood felt on me, and the way Mab's violence against her seemed so much more horrific than against any of the others. I'd been willing to divert Mab's attention away from her, even knowing it meant that someone else would fill the vacancy she left and become a plaything. Maybe it was the way she reminded me of the Mab I'd known when we were younger. Maybe it was the possibility that she could be the only *good* to come from the sunshine girl who had been one of my closest friends.

I wanted to protect her from the darkness that had consumed

her mother, to take her out of the shadows so that she could feel the sun on her face. Mab would never allow Rheaghan to take his niece home with him, but she trusted *me*, and that meant I carried the weight of her fate on my shoulders.

I knew I should make my way downstairs for breakfast, allow Rheaghan to talk me out of the decision I'd already made and fought to deny. But I couldn't, wouldn't, be able to stop thinking of her and the strength she'd shown where others might have broken. I wasn't able to just simply let things be when Mab had continued to torment her in the days that had passed since Rheaghan and I had successfully intervened. Rheaghan had continuously tried and failed to convince his sister to show her own daughter mercy since, and the tales of her suffering had spread around Tar Mesa, reaching me even as I tried to stay away from her.

The need to do what I could to protect her from this fate was overwhelming, even if I sensed it was her own stubbornness that prevented her from giving Mab what she wanted and sparing herself the pain of Mab's attention.

Rage building in my chest, I tore open my bedroom door and stepped into the hallway, only to find Malachi approaching my room. "The Queen bids you to join her in her bedroom," he said, and the command struck me deep in the chest. I swallowed, everything within me sinking into a pit. I had counted myself fortunate that in the centuries since I'd come to know the Queen of Air and Darkness, she had not yet summoned me to her bed.

I nodded in spite of myself, the daunting horror of what might wait for me in her chambers overshadowed by reality. As if being forced to entertain Mab wasn't bad enough, and didn't fill me with revulsion that made everything within me wither, the knowledge that it would make my relationship with her daughter *awkward* at best was an added complication I hadn't foreseen.

The walk through the halls was both too slow and too quick, leaving me with little hope that I had been summoned for any reason but what I anticipated. Mab was not known for conducting business within her room, only those she summoned for entertainment joining her and her friend, Malazan, in the space they considered private.

Her doors were intricately shaped metal, carved with flowers and thorns. Malachi knocked on the surface three times.

"Enter," Mab's voice said, sinking into me and feeling like a death sentence. Malachi responded by pushing the door open, revealing my first glimpse of the inside of Mab's private quarters. Snakes covered the floor between the door and the opulent bed that rested against the other wall, the intricately carved, gilded headboard shimmering against waves of light fabric that lined the walls. The space was as opulent as I'd expected, but it had been filled with traces of warmth and Summer Court touches that I hadn't.

For the first time, I understood what Rheaghan meant when he claimed his sister was still in there somewhere. Her bedroom was a sanctuary loaded with items that would have reminded a young girl of the home she'd left behind. Whereas Mab decorated the rest of her court with cold, unfeeling touches of stone and iron and all the things that made it feel as empty as it was large, her rooms were smaller and far more personal than anything I could have foreseen. The thought made me uncomfortable, and I shifted from side to side before I caught myself.

I simultaneously wanted to believe that the girl I'd known was still in there and capable of being saved, and that she would never have to know the truth of what she'd become and the things she'd done.

I cleared my throat as Mab sat on her bed, petting one of her snakes on the underside of his head.

Do snakes have chins?

"You wished to see me, my Queen?" I asked, watching as her only friend, Malazan, made her way from the dining table to perch on the edge of the bed. Her stare was intent on me as she leaned back on her hands, attempting to present a seductive figure.

It elicited the opposite reaction from me, making everything wither and shrink at the possibility that it could be either of them who had wanted me to join them in their private quarters.

Mab waved her hand and the snakes that remained in my direct path slithered to the side, creating an aisle that I could navigate carefully to approach the two Fae women. I took the first step, knowing that it would do me no good to delay the inevitable.

The unfortunate reality of the situation was that it did not matter if I did not desire either of them; to reject them would be a death sentence. The only line they did not cross and did not toy with was the one created by a mate bond, and even that was simply because a man's body could not and would not react in such a way that they would find useful.

The bond prevented it entirely, though I had no doubt there had been a time when they did it purely for torturous purposes. They'd found other ways to engage those interests, though, other ways to make their victims scream.

"How long has it been since they brought me *my daughter*?" she asked when I finally stood at the foot of her bed. The topic of conversation made everything in me both still and surge with relief, and I hoped that she had not brought me here to fill her bed.

"A couple weeks, if I had to guess, my Queen," I said, attempting to keep my voice calm. Half interested.

I was completely unable to count the nights I had spent sleepless and wondering what I could do to help us both get what we wanted—what we *needed*. Fallon needed freedom from the overbearing, controlling, and outright abusive mother she'd found herself imprisoned by.

I just needed her.

"And yet she has proven herself to be entirely useless. Tell me, Etan," she said, gritting her teeth through her disappointment. Malazan reached out and stroked Mab's knee over the top of her dress, and while the movement wasn't sexual in the slightest, it hinted at the intimacy between the two of them. Out of everyone in this world, Malazan was perhaps the only person Mab would miss if she were to disappear from her life. "Do I seem like the kind of queen to trifle with?"

"Of course not, my Queen," I said, bowing my head slightly to indicate my respect. "Do you have any reason to believe that Maeve is defying you intentionally?"

Mab tilted her head to the side, as if it had not occurred to her that there could be any reason other than defiance that motivated Fallon's actions. "You think *my daughter* is truly unable to access her magic?" she asked, releasing the snake who had cuddled up with her. It slithered onto the floor, gliding its way off the high, opulent bed and joining the rest of its kind in a pile on the floor for warmth. Most children of the Gods were born with only a sliver of magic in their veins, and the only reason Mab believed that Fallon would be different was her own hubris.

"I do not pretend to know Maeve at all, so I cannot make any statements about what may be her motivations. But what I do know is that I have watched you break the strongest of men to your will. Your methods are effective, even if messy at times, and for Maeve to be able to resist that would be most unexpected when she does not seem to have lived a violent life in Nothrek," I explained, allowing that to sink in. The next part would need to be handled carefully, because Mab would not take well to me insinuating that her daughter could be anything other than powerful. She did not see herself as just another of the many Gods and Goddesses that had been born to the Primordials.

She saw herself as the Queen of them all. Even going so far as to ignore the fact that the magic that gave her the ability to overpower the rest of her kind wasn't the magic that flowed through her veins.

It was the product of the crown that had cursed her to the darkness.

"At the very least, her magic should be acting defensively without her even willing it to happen. While she may be fully grown, her magic is new to her. I have a difficult time believing she has mastered control like this in a matter of weeks, when it takes most Fae decades," I said, keeping my words as vague as possible. If Mab knew I'd been watching Fallon too closely, even as I tried to avoid her, if she knew how I listened to every whisper that carried her name, she would never allow me to influence her choices regarding her daughter.

She'd see me as biased, rather than an impartial advisor whose opinion she could trust.

"What other explanation could there be?" Malazan asked, her singsongy voice deceptively sweet as she eyed me up and down.

I swallowed back my discomfort, hoping that the other woman wouldn't express desires to Mab.

If this court held one rule, it was that Malazan got whatever, and whomever, she wanted, outside of those who were already mated. A gift from her Queen for her unwavering loyalty.

"Perhaps Maeve's powers could reasonably lean more toward her Summer Court heritage than her Shadow Court heritage, and her lack of exposure to those elements could be restraining her to some extent," I said. I hoped more than anything that Mab couldn't see through the bullshit that I fed her, but even if I had no precedent to make me believe that the words I spoke were entirely true, they didn't feel like a half-truth.

It was entirely possible that Fallon's inability to sit in the sun or bask in the heat of the Summer Court beaches was weakening the magic that she should have had at her fingertips.

You could not play with what you did not know.

"You think going to the Summer Court will strengthen her hold if she does follow in her grandmother's footsteps?" Malazan asked, raising a brow. It shouldn't have come as a surprise if she did lean toward her grandmother's magic, given that both of Khaos's children with Diell had done so, oddly enough.

"I don't think it could hurt to find out. But given that Rheaghan cannot be trusted to guide Maeve in a direction you would approve of, I am uncertain how it would be at all possible under the circumstances," I said, knowing that Mab would never allow such a thing. She was far too paranoid to give Rheaghan any kind of control, believing that he would do whatever it took to undermine her from a distance.

"No," Mab agreed, rising to the occasion as I'd thought she might. "Rheaghan cannot be trusted with Maeve."

"But perhaps there is another way I could send her to the Summer Court," she mused, turning her attention to where Malazan waited at her side. The other woman smirked, as if reading Mab's thoughts.

"I would of course be happy to watch over her for you, my Queen. But as I am not related to her, I would have no control over her once we left Tar Mesa. She would fall under her uncle's jurisdiction by blood right," I said, resisting the urge to fidget with my fingers.

"Though, Maeve has proven to be an effective way to motivate Estrella to do as I wish, so I must admit my hesitation to lose her as a bargaining chip," Mab thought out loud, standing from the bed to pace the floor of her bedroom. Her snakes moved out of her way with each step she took, moving with her in a fluid, natural dance that shouldn't have been possible. "I would need for her to be supervised by someone I could trust to bring her home at a moment's notice."

"What about a husband?" Malazan asked, shrugging her shoulders as Mab turned to look at her with wide, mocking eyes. The thought had already occurred to her. "Her husband would be responsible for her even above an uncle. Rheaghan may still be the King of Summer for the time being, but even he wouldn't interfere with marriage. Betroth Maeve to a Summer Court Fae and send her home with him after the Tithe. She'll get to experience the magic of the Summer Court and still be under your influence. Maybe we'll be lucky and she'll return with magic so she can be of use," she added, making Mab's lips purse in thought.

"It could work," Mab said finally. Her eyes snagged on mine as she turned to look at me, the depths of them churning as she thought through her options. "But who would I choose?"

Malazan slid her hand over Mab's arm, stroking her skin in that affectionate, almost sisterly way that she'd adopted to manipulate her Queen. Her gaze remained fixed on me, a knowing there that said so much that we had never spoken in words.

We saw one another for what we were, for the ways that we guided Mab in directions that served our purpose. She knew exactly what I'd intended when I started this line of thinking, and she could derail me entirely.

"There is only one logical choice, my Queen," she said, her voice practically a purr. I tensed, waiting for the moment of truth and not knowing which direction I hoped she took. Her support of me as Fallon's husband would come at a cost. "Etan is your most loyal Summer Court Fae. Should something happen to Rheaghan, it only makes sense that his chosen heir should be married to Maeve. Now that she's returned, she is the rightful heir to the Summer Court. You would erase any conflict that may arise if people were to question who should rule under these circumstances with Maeve being so newly returned to us," Malazan added, her smirk meant only for me.

"The heir and the spare," Mab said with a returning grin.

"Me? I never had any intention of marrying—" I argued, wanting to dissuade any preconceived notion that this might have been an intentional result on my part.

"It's settled. You will marry my daughter. The bonds of marriage have long since been used to establish and strengthen alliances, and you will solidify my claim to the Summer Court through Maeve. I'll inform my daughter of your pending nuptials soon enough, and after the Tithe is complete you'll be able to take her home."

I swallowed, bowing at the waist with a flourish as a sheepish smile claimed my face. "You honor me, my Queen," I said. My gaze met Malazan's for a brief moment when I straightened, her gaze knowing.

Well played, she seemed to say.

She'd need to be dealt with eventually, but for now, I let myself revel in the victory of the moment as I returned to my room to wait for the announcement to be made.

For Fallon to know she'd be mine.

Four

FALLON

I worried the bridge of my nose between my fingers, hating this relentless game we played. As far as Mab knew, there was no magic within me—making me a complete abomination to everything she believed her daughter should possess. I didn't own her penchant for darkness or her cruelty, only an extreme distaste for the place that was destined to be my home.

I was Mab's only heir, but she was too far lost to her disillusion to see that I would *never* sit upon the throne. Even if she'd known about the magic Imelda kept at bay, the only way Mab would hand down her rule was if she lay dead and her soul was lost to the Void. She would have no control over her heir continuing to hold power in her death, and the Court of Shadows would return to the rightful line of inheritance.

The throne would belong to Caldris, and I would *gladly* hand it over. I might not have known where I belonged or if such a place even existed, but I knew it wasn't here.

Estrella entered the throne room behind me, everything in my being sensing her proximity. She and I were the same, some gnarled and twisted-up bond. Opposites, but in a way that felt like two halves of one whole.

I turned to the side, letting our eyes meet as she took in the situation before her. I watched that all-seeing gaze track over the male across from me. I'd seen him only in passing moments in the halls of Tar Mesa, aside from the two times he'd offered aid in the throne room, but that stare always seemed to study me too intently. Even now, with Mab to witness the curiosity that could never mean anything good, his head tilted to the side in thought, as if I were a puzzle he couldn't quite solve.

Estrella's eyes narrowed into a glare as she raised her chin higher, that protective streak making everything in her go taut. In this place of darkness, enemies were everywhere and nothing and *no one* was innocent.

I resisted the urge to laugh, knowing that Estrella would think nothing of severing his head from his body if she thought he meant me harm. It wouldn't matter to her that the man was Rheagan's second-in-command—placed in his position by Mab herself to spy on her brother when he remained in the Summer Court. Etan's mouth curved at one corner, the faintest hint of a smirk rising in response to the smile I quelled. His deep auburn hair hung around his shoulders in choppy, layered waves—his brown eyes cold and unyielding in spite of the amusement to the curve of his mouth.

As if he could feel Estrella's disapproval, he turned to face her finally as she came to stand beside me. She stared down Etan and his master, my mother, like the queen I knew she was meant to be. One day she would have that title—would rule at Caldris's side, not as a pretty ornament, but as an equal, because there was no one and nothing in this world that could put Estrella Barlowe into a cage.

I knew it as surely as I knew my own name. She'd been born to break her chains and use them to strangle her abusers.

"You summoned me?" she asked, refusing to bow where any others would quiver in their boots at the thought of showing Mab such disrespect. We hadn't been in Tar Mesa for long, but I knew Estrella was the only one who could get away with such insolence.

She was a curiosity to Mab, a game she very much enjoyed playing with.

"I tire of having two incompetent children beneath my roof. You cannot seem to summon the magic that we both know you possess, magic that would make you *useful*. Maeve cannot seem to summon *any* magic at all. Both are unacceptable to me," Mab said, running her tongue over her teeth in dissatisfaction. She made a sucking noise in the side of her cheek, as if her annoyance was not already obvious.

"Her name is Fallon," Estrella corrected, holding Mab's glare with one of her own. It would never cease to amaze me that after centuries of separation from her own flesh and bone, I was nothing more than something to be used. There was no love in Mab's heart for her long-lost daughter.

Only disappointment.

"But I fail to see what you would like either of us to do. Magic cannot be forced. If it does not come when summoned, then perhaps we are not fit to control it," Estrella continued, utilizing her unique ability to come very close to outright lying. I hadn't retained that skill after my transformation upon arriving in Alfheimr. I had very much become defined by and limited to the rules that the Fae had to navigate, hinting further at the fact that we did not know *what* Estrella was. The *only* reason I'd been able to tell Mab I possessed no magic was because it was a half-truth.

There was *something* stirring within me, but Imelda suppressed it before I could ever touch that magic and allow it to breathe.

Mab sneered and huffed a laugh at Estrella, a grim, bitter smile transforming her face. She should have been beautiful, *was* beautiful, but the ugliness within her shone through her every expression and the crazed, desperate look that always seemed to linger in her eyes. "I might have believed that to be true if I hadn't heard rumors of all the things you've done. If I hadn't *seen* them in your memories and for myself, Little Mouse." The Queen of Air and Darkness's voice was low and soft, for she had no need to raise it to invoke terror in most who came into her presence.

"I think I have proven myself to be more than a mouse," Estrella said, smiling in the face of what most feared. After her battle with the Minotaur in the Labyrinth, no one could deny that she'd proven herself to be far more than a rodent scurrying in the dark. I wrung my hands together, one fingertip touching the teardrop mark that bound Estrella and me to one another. I could only hope that some of her bravery would bleed into my skin, become mine as much as it was hers. Most of my life had been spent waiting and hiding, tolerating uncomfortable situations but never risking myself.

Aside from that night the cave beast attacked me, I'd never known violence before coming to Tar Mesa. I'd thought myself brave all those nights I'd spent in the tunnels of the rebellion, longing to step foot in the sun and fight in battles I had no place in. Only now did I see the beauty I'd been offered, that Imelda and my human family had provided me with.

"Occasionally, the mouse's bite carries a deadly disease. But it is still just a mouse, at the end of the day," Mab said. I watched Estrella's jaw tense as she swallowed back her rage at the insult. She drew it within her, storing it for motivation later when the time was right.

At first glance, I would think Estrella impulsive, that her small aggressions toward Mab were parts of her that should have been contained. But I knew her better, and saw the deep well of rage that existed within her. The comments she made and the fights were nothing compared to what she stored for later, and Mab would be wise to fear the day that Estrella could act on that anger in truth.

"What do you want from us?" Estrella asked, glancing at me. I saw the drive there, the need to protect me against any and all threats. I felt the same, but whereas I felt limited in what I could offer while keeping the growing magic within me a secret, Estrella's strength knew no bounds. She would suffer. She would hurt. She would walk to the ends of the earth if it meant saving me from the fate she'd already been forced to endure in Tar Mesa. While Mab had tortured me to attempt to draw out my power, it was nothing compared to what I'd witnessed her doing to my friend.

Estrella's strength came in fighting, and it showed. Mine had always been in secrecy.

"I only have the energy to invest my time into one of you. I have no desire to make that decision, so the two of you will determine who remains here with me," Mab said, waving a hand as if it were inconsequential to her. My heart dropped into my stomach, even though I'd already known she hadn't cared for me in the slightest. The confirmation that she would send me away if I was less useful than Estrella was still a swift kick to the gut and made me miss the human parents who had loved me all the more.

It was also a relief at the same time.

"Will the one who does not stay go free?" Estrella asked, sensing the trap in Mab's offer. There was no way she would ever allow anyone to escape her clutches freely; rather, she would kill whomever she did not keep. But I would gladly die if it meant Estrella had a chance to live with Caldris, to know serenity and peace with the love of her life.

All I wanted was freedom. Freedom to roam and discover the

world I'd been kept from all my life. Being trapped in Tar Mesa with Mab meant I had only exchanged one prison for another, and I was so tired of cages.

I wanted to live a life I chose without fear of having it ripped away from me.

"Of course not," Mab said with a cruel laugh. "Etan is in need of a wife, and is owed one for the loyalty he has shown me during my brother's reign as King. Whoever does not remain with me shall be betrothed to him and return to the Summer Court with him after the Tithe."

Estrella's eyes widened, her arm twitching at her side as if she meant to raise it in shock. She twisted her head, her jaw working as if she'd swallowed a rock and needed to force it down. "I have a mate," she said, turning to look at Etan cautiously. He shifted uncomfortably, clearly bothered by the idea of taking another man's mate as his wife.

"It is adorable that you think I care about such trivialities. Political marriages happen all the time. Caldris will learn to share you and remember his place," Mab said, dismissing the notion that acting outside of the mating bond would be *agonizing*. For both Estrella and Caldris. There would be no pleasure in being bound to another man, only suffering and pain. While Estrella likely wouldn't have to share Etan's bed in a political marriage, the separation and very notion of being bonded to another in any way went against the conventions of the Fae.

But Mab didn't care, because she was just as likely to murder a mate out of spite. Love and mate bonds held no power over her.

Estrella smiled through the pain, and I knew she was confronted with the images of the carnage Caldris would unleash if anyone even attempted to claim her as his. "I somehow doubt that," she scoffed. She turned her head, her face twisted with sadness. I knew she didn't want to leave me to that fate, but that was the only path forward.

"It's okay, Estrella," I said, my eyes filling with tears. The thought of leaving her here, of abandoning her to this place that was so determined to break her, was enough to tear me in half.

She shook her head, pursing her lips to fight back tears of her own.

"Whoever displays the magic I wish to see first will stay here with me," Mab said, interrupting our moment.

"And if neither of us do?" Estrella asked, prepared to simply refuse to make the choice. If neither of us chose, would we simply continue on as we already had been? How long could we keep going that way?

"Then I'll marry the other one of you off to one of my other allies. Perhaps a far crueler one than Etan. I have done you a kindness in selecting him. He is not a cruel man and will not be a cruel husband. He is distant and pragmatic, but will see that your needs are met. I would tolerate nothing less for my daughter," Mab said, turning to me with a knowing stare. "Even if she does not obey me."

She knew beyond a shadow of the Veil that I would be the one she sent to this marriage. She knew it would be Estrella who displayed her power and remained behind, hoping and waiting for the moment when she and Caldris could be free together. She knew, and she was willing to sacrifice me to force Estrella's hand and drive distance between us by putting us in charge of the decision.

After centuries of searching, I'd proven to be a waste of effort. A waste of time.

The Veil had been erected to keep us from Mab, to protect us from being raised in her image.

And for what?

I stepped forward, turning my back to Mab and placing myself between her and Estrella. I took my friend's hands in my own, stroking my thumb over the circle on the back of her hand. I ran my touch over the Fae Mark, the reminder of the bond that mattered more than ours, summoning that connection to the surface to remind Estrella of everything I was willing to sacrifice myself for.

Etan would not ever love me because I was not his mate, and I could not possibly love a man who would willingly align himself with Mab. With every day that passed, it became more and more clear that there was no love for me, not the kind that Estrella had found with Caldris.

She deserved to have what she had already found and suffered for, and there was always a chance that Etan and I could come to our own arrangement. Maybe he could allow me to have some form of freedom so long as I didn't interfere with his plans. Maybe my place as his wife would allow me to at least travel through Alfheimr, even if it didn't offer freedom in the truest sense. Whatever he offered, there was every chance it would be better than Tar Mesa.

My palm touched the white teardrop of our blood vow on her hand, and the pulse of magic spread through me at the same moment Estrella shivered.

"It's okay," I said, my hand trailing up the white marks on her forearm. My fingers tingled with warmth, as if my touch alone could bring forth the magic she fought to suppress and keep hidden from Mab.

She shook her head again, the denial rising on her lips. "I can't," she protested.

"You can," I said, touching my forehead to hers. I pressed forward, my eyes holding hers and willing her to see the truth. Her bottom lip quivered, her desperation to protect me at war with her need to be with her mate. All my life, people had been protecting me from danger—they'd been doing whatever it took to keep me tucked away and safe, guarding my light that was too good to be sacrificed to the darkness of this world. All I could do was try to be worthy of that sacrifice. It was too late to hide Estrella's powers from Mab, but we could still hide mine, and I felt in my bones that was the path I was meant to take.

That was how I could be worthy.

Beyond Estrella's need to protect me was a greater doubt, though, and I read it in every line of Estrella's face. In the tension at her temples, the crinkling at the corner of her mouth as she forced a frown that was unnatural to her pretty face. Her fear—of what Mab would do with her magic. Her fear of what she herself was capable of. "It is you. The most terrifying part of you, but it's also the most beautiful. All you have to do is let it out."

"It's not that simple," Estrella said, resisting the urge to make eye contact with Mab. Even our words came too close to revealing the truth, Estrella's painful efforts to keep her secrets safe useless in the face of a woman who would do anything to learn them.

I turned her away from Mab and guided her out of the throne room. Mab and Etan followed behind us, and I knew we were both aware of the fact that we were only able to exit the palace of Tar Mesa because she allowed it. That the guards standing at the entrance would have impaled us on sight if she so much as breathed a word of discontent. Instead, the Queen of Air and Darkness seemed satisfied to allow the situation to play out, watching with only a mild curiosity.

"She cannot use you for evil if you do not allow it. Knowledge is power, but do you really think anything she does is stronger than you?" I asked, my voice a low murmur to keep the moment private between us. "You have lived in fear of what you are. You have suffered the pain of suppressing yourself to protect the world. When will you learn that you are not our destruction, Estrella? You are our savior."

Estrella's knees buckled as we stepped outside, the moons shining high in the sky above us. My bare arms warmed from them as I took a step back with a nod. I released Estrella, and she turned to watch Mab and Etan as they waited for her decision.

"I'm not strong enough for this," she said.

"Then lean on the people who love you. Take what you need from us," I said, raising a hand. She stared down at the threads she saw in everything, the ways she interpreted the world that the rest of us could not. Nodding, she allowed her eyes to drift closed as she sank into herself, into the well of power that I felt rise up to meet her. Goose bumps rose along my arms in response to the feel of it on my skin, forcing me to hold my ground. I couldn't risk Estrella seeing me back away from her, couldn't risk her thinking I was afraid of her.

Mab studied Estrella intently as she wrapped something between her fingers, curling it around her flesh as silent tears rolled down her cheeks. She stared up at the sky with wide eyes, as if she saw the world for the very first time.

Estrella closed her palm, pressing her fingers into it slowly. I followed her gaze to the sky, watching as one of the moons winked out of existence as if it had never been there at all. She reached up with her other hand as Mab gasped, the shock in her voice bringing a smile of pure joy to my face as I stared up at that one lone moon. Estrella gathered more threads into that hand, snuffing out the light and plunging the night sky into darkness. The other moon vanished, the stars disappearing along with it, until a dark like I'd never known surrounded me.

The complete absence of light was suffocating, making my breaths come harsher and more quickly. Only the light of fires hanging from the doorway of the palace illuminated the ground before it, and I pointed my stare at them and fixated on that single source of light.

"Impossible," Mab whispered, taking a step toward Estrella.

Estrella turned to face her, unflinching when the Queen of Air and Darkness cupped her cheeks and stared down at her. There was a cross between horror and awe in that stare, and she ran her thumb through the tears on Estrella's cheeks in a mockery of gentleness that felt all wrong coming from her.

"And yet here I am," Estrella murmured, drawing back from Mab. She released the threads, tossing her hands into the sky so that the moons reclaimed their rightful place. "Did that give you the answers you were so desperate for?"

"You can see the threads of fate," Mab said, her voice filled with awe as she stared down at Estrella's hands. "That is how you summon."

Shock coursed through me with the realization that Mab knew what she shouldn't, that she'd recognized the way Estrella touched the world. "You see them, too?" Estrella asked, swallowing so loudly I heard it.

"I see . . . shadows of them. Whispers on the wind occasionally, but I can never grasp them. I'm not—" Mab paused, clearing her throat as the closest thing I'd ever seen to emotion clogged it.

"You're not what?" Estrella asked. She was so close to answers that I took an unwilling step toward her, pausing only so I would not interrupt the moment. I wouldn't be the one to keep her from the answers she needed desperately.

Mab clenched her jaw, and I could already imagine the strategy working through her head. The plans she was making for how she could use this knowledge, and Estrella, to her greatest advantage.

"A Primordial," Mab answered finally, knocking the breath from my lungs.

Estrella was a *Primordial*?

Five

ETAN

I stared at the woman in shock, the impossibility of her existence contradicted before my very eyes. The Primordials had locked themselves away, disappeared from the world centuries prior to her existence, from the kernels of information I'd been able to gather from my conversations with Mab and those who were the most loyal to her. Estrella Barlowe should not have possessed the power that Mab claimed to have witnessed, the assertion in the voice of the Queen of Air and Darkness stealing the breath from my lungs. There was the faintest of tremors to it, the sound so unlike anything I'd ever heard from the Goddess who feared nothing and no one that I felt my head tip to the side as I turned it to stare at her profile.

Estrella and Fallon seemed oblivious to the note of fear that made her voice shake, their knowledge of her short-lived. They didn't have centuries at her side to understand the implication of that fear and what it would mean for Estrella.

She'd been in danger since the moment she'd stepped foot in

Alfheimr, but Mab would never allow something she feared to continue living. It was only a matter of time before she figured out the best way to eliminate the threat Estrella posed, only a matter of time before she did what she could to rid herself of the competition for power, so no other could challenge her.

There were two sides to Mab. The one that everyone saw, the crazed madwoman who acted without fear of consequences and hurt anyone who stood in her way. That was the Queen who had nothing to fear; no one could right her wrongs or avenge their families. That was the woman who had been driven to a cruel, evil glee at the suffering of others. Most assumed her incapable of control, of containing that side of herself to play the long game when it was necessary to her survival.

But I'd seen her do just that with Caldris, keeping him contained for centuries when he might have otherwise been able to fight back and claim what was his by birthright. She'd taken her greatest opposition and turned him into her greatest weapon, but whereas Caldris had been a child when he consented to the snake wrapped around his heart, Estrella was a woman. She understood the implications of such a thing, and fully grasped the fact that there were some fates worse than death.

The glare she graced Mab with was confirmation of that, a promise that she would fight her until the very end. That glare was her death sentence, Mab's answering smirk her affirmation of a fate signed, sealed, and all but delivered to the Fates themselves.

Movement at my side caught my eye, pulling my stare away from the standoff occurring before me. Had it been anyone else, nothing could have torn me away from the gravity of this moment. From the implication that the future of Fae kind would be decided when these two women decided to go to war.

Only one creature could tempt me from keeping a wary eye on the two women.

My future wife.

Fallon raised her chin, her strong, angular jaw set as her full mouth parted into a gleeful smile. It was in that moment that I saw the resemblance between her and her mother, the deep, devastating beauty that felt too dangerous to grasp. I didn't know that I would ever be able to contain it, to hold her in my arms in spite of the position she would soon play in my life. She was the kind of beauty that slipped through your fingers, disappearing into the wind like a mirage that couldn't possibly be real.

I'd seen her at court before this moment, silent and stoic at Mab's side in spite of the atrocities her mother committed, in spite of the pain she inflicted on her own daughter in an effort to gain the answers she sought. But Fallon refused any and all attention, gave no answers and showed no signs of the power that she *must* have had on even a small level, given her lineage.

The moon played off her fair skin, such a contrast to Estrella's bronze and my own, which was deeply tanned by the sun in my home court. She looked as if she'd been locked away in a tower without a window, as if her skin had never been given the privilege of stepping into the sunlight, of feeling that warmth on the cool tone of her complexion.

As if she felt my attention, she turned to face me. The smile drifted off her stunning face slowly, her pouty lips pressing into a tight line. Her disapproval should have discouraged me, or at the very least made me wary of the kind of marriage we might have now that the betrothal was set in stone.

Instead, it brought an answering smile to my face, amusement flickering through me like candlelight. While the Fae couldn't *lie*, few were so outright with their honesty to allow their every thought and feeling to show upon their face.

Watching Fallon think was like reading the pages of an open book, the words written in neat script for all to see. The very thought of getting to know *all* her expressions was a promise that would taunt me until it came to fruition.

Even in her disapproval, I'd never seen a mouth so perfectly shaped, her top and bottom lips evenly thick to the point of looking like they had been painted on. Her lips were deeper than was natural, nearly the color of blood against her pale skin. I'd always thought the color of Mab's lips was the effect of painting them with the blood of her enemies, but Fallon contradicted that notion.

I felt certain she only had one enemy in this world, and that was the Queen who had so easily dismissed her in favor of Estrella.

Fallon crossed her arms over her chest, and where another woman might have looked insecure in the motion, she squared her shoulders as she studied me and found me wanting. The set to that strong jaw indicated the fight I would have on my hands, her entire body tense as she waited for abuse. Her hazel eyes bored into mine, her hair so dark it was nearly black.

"Sorry to disappoint you," she said, her mouth parting ever so slightly. Her teeth peeked through, bright white and perfectly straight, with only the tiniest of gaps between the two front teeth, which felt too innocent for a woman staring at me with such disdain.

"Disappoint me?" I asked, meeting her pointed stare. Most withered under intense eye contact, feeling uncomfortable with the aspect of self-confidence in a world determined to tear us down. The eyes were a window to the soul, a reminder that our bodies were nothing but flesh, and that the real pain came from within.

"Estrella is far too important to marry the likes of you, no matter how beautiful you may find her," Fallon said, earning a grin from me. A grin that I usually suppressed when trapped in this court of darkness and gloom.

"She is beautiful," I said, taking a step toward my future wife. The one who had been so willing to save her friend that she'd sacrificed herself to an arrangement, to a loveless marriage decided by the mother she hated so clearly. That hatred extended to me as well, if her glare was any indication. I raised my hand from my side slowly, watching as she finally broke eye contact to study the movement. She stood her ground, lifting her chin as my fingers ghosted over it. My thumb found her bottom lip, the plump flesh parting as I drew it down to get a glimpse of her teeth again.

I wanted her smile, the devious grin that had graced her face at the prospect of Estrella besting the Queen of Air and Darkness, who Fallon believed me loyal to. Instead, she bared her teeth at me, jerking her head back from my touch. I let her go, running my tongue over my bottom teeth as her snarl gave me my first glimpse of her pointed little fangs at the corner of her mouth.

"But I am far from disappointed, Princess," I said, holding out a hand and leaning forward into a courtly half bow. Fallon sucked her cheek inward, hollowing out her face slightly and making her angular features even more striking in her distaste for me. She cast one last glance toward Mab and Estrella, the two of them staring upward toward the night sky. With a sigh, she lifted her hand and placed it in mine, allowing me to draw her into my side and escort her back to the palace of Tar Mesa. We took a few steps, ascending the stairs and entering the doors that the guards pulled open with a dramatic flourish. "I am far more concerned with understanding why you believe Estrella to be any more important than you are," I said, continuing our conversation in the absence of Mab's prying ears.

Fallon scoffed, her condescending sneer making me want nothing more than to wipe it off her beautiful face. She'd come to learn that her attitude would never be met with violence, not with me, but I would still show her all the ways I could own her.

She would just enjoy them.

"*Everyone* is worth less than Estrella," she said as we climbed the stairs, casually leading me to the rooms she'd been given as hers during her time in Tar Mesa. At the time, she'd probably thought this would be her final home—that she would either remain here as her mother's prisoner or die here. Instead, she'd know the grand opulence of the Summer Court, of breezy fabrics and bathing pools with flowing water in every room carved into the hillside that kept us sheltered from the worst of the sandstorms. "It isn't an insult to myself to admit as much. I would not necessarily say the same of another."

"Perhaps she is worth more to *you*, but I will not allow you to make less of your importance. No matter the circumstances that led us here, you are to be my wife now, and I'll not allow anyone to insult you. Not even you," I said, pausing in front of the door at the end of the hall. Fallon faced me, expressionless, as if she couldn't decide how to react to my statement.

"You don't have to pretend that you care. You don't even know me, and we both know this marriage will be nothing more than a political arrangement," she said, her voice soft. It was her reminder to herself, of exactly what this was, and I appreciated that she wanted to go into our situation with clearly defined roles.

"Is that so?" I asked, raising the hand that did not hold hers and touching my thumb to her cheek. I dragged it over her high cheekbone, reveling in the tiny hitch of breath that caught in her lungs.

"What else could it possibly be?" she asked, her whisper barely audible in the abandoned hallway.

I shrugged, taking my hand back and releasing hers from the hold of my other hand. "It may be an *arrangement*," I said, emphasizing the word she'd chosen. "But that doesn't mean we cannot enjoy said arrangement." Fallon had no way of knowing what I'd done, or realizing that I'd been the one to put the idea in Mab's head. Playing games with Mab was a strategy, a slowly evolving plan to make her believe the decision had been hers and hers alone, and that offered me anonymity where Fallon was concerned. If she knew the truth, I had no doubt she would fault me for her newfound situation, even if I'd done it with her well-being in mind.

Mostly.

Fallon did not yet know how to play that game, but I'd had

centuries of manipulating the Queen of Air and Darkness to benefit my people. Fallon would be the first time I used that ability for something that wasn't entirely selfless, arranging a wedding that Fallon had played right into. I would keep her safe, and that eased some of the niggling guilt I felt over what I hoped to gain in the process.

I placed my hand on the handle to her door, turning it and shoving the door open before stepping out of her way. It was a room I'd spent my fair share of time in, getting to know Fallon through the space she kept as her own when she was gone and I was attempting to avoid her presence in Mab's court.

She moved to pass me, making her way through the door and pausing only when I leaned in and placed my mouth at her ear. "And you will enjoy it," I added, stepping back from her suddenly as she gave me a wide-eyed stare. She drew in a deep breath, her shock palpable as she moved into her room on shaky legs.

She didn't so much as meet my stare as she swung the door closed behind her, sealing herself off into her place of false safety.

I grinned at the back of the door, running a palm over the wooden surface before I turned on my heel and stalked toward my own rooms.

The best part of hunting within the Shadow Court?

My *wife* wasn't going anywhere.

Six

FALLON

Days passed without me needing to spend time with Etan, confirming my assumption that we would have a marriage in name only. Any man who actually cared to know a thing about the woman he was set to marry would have spent his time getting to know me, not actively avoiding me. I was grateful that he was matching my energy and going about his business as if nothing had changed.

It soothed something within me, the part that resisted the notion of another cage. The last thing I wanted was a man who thought to contain and control me, keeping me caged in a court that I had no desire to exist within. I would be free to do as I pleased, and so would the male that was too handsome for his own good.

I made my way through the grand entry that led to the throne room, ignoring the warmth of his brown eyes as they wandered to me briefly. Just as quickly, he shifted his attention back to Rheaghan and dismissed me from his focus.

Good.

The King of Summer smiled at me, his expression warm and unguarded. He'd come to me sporadically in the last couple of days, showing interest in knowing his sister's daughter, but even the knowledge that I would be spending more time with my uncle couldn't make me embrace the concept of a relationship with him.

Not here, not when Mab would so readily use it as a weakness. If I was to return with him and Etan to the Summer Court, we would have plenty of time to get to know one another.

The doors to the throne room were closed, indicating that whatever Mab was doing within the closed space, she had no desire for company at this moment. I sighed, glancing around the hall and debating what to do with myself in the meantime. It was no secret that Mab wanted me to be available to her whenever she dictated, but the closed door offered me a rare bit of freedom, and she had no care for what I did with my time when she didn't require my presence.

My eyes once again strayed toward Etan. His hair was the deepest auburn, so dark that the red was almost drowned out by the depth of the brown undertone. He continued to ignore my presence in favor of socializing among the Gods who were present at the court. It should have pleased me to avoid his notice, and on some level, it did. I wanted the freedom that came from being ignored, but that freedom would mean nothing to me if I allowed the bonds of our betrothal to keep me controlled regardless.

I was not a woman who would fall quietly into subservience. I was not a woman who would ever allow herself to be owned, especially not by a man who could not even be bothered to publicly acknowledge me. It wasn't Etan alone who needed the reminder of exactly what this was; I did, too. We were both free to do as we pleased.

Imelda would tell me I was being petty and defiant to my own detriment.

Fortunately, I hadn't seen the witch in days, and that voice in my head was barely a whisper of warning.

I turned my attention to the males he spoke to, tipping my head to the side as I observed them. The man on his other side, opposite Rheaghan, had hair the color of deep night itself. His eyes shone out of his fair skin, a pale silver with the slightest hint of pink to them. His gaze trailed down my body where I stood in the gown Pax had dressed me in, believing it would please Mab to see me in the colors of the Shadow Court so willingly.

I felt that gaze rake over me from head to toe, snagging at the line of cleavage the deep neckline left open to his perusal. I smirked when those pale eyes finally found mine once more, gliding forward as he stepped off the wall where he'd stood beside my betrothed.

He met me in the center of the entryway, his playful grin making my own mouth spread into a matching smile. "Princess," he said, bowing his head forward in a show of respect that we both knew I hadn't earned.

"I'm at the disadvantage of not knowing you," I said, cocking my head to the side as I reached out with a single hand and patted his chest, adjusting the collar of his tunic where it had folded over the line of his dress coat.

"Soren. God of Twilight," he answered, reaching up to grasp my hand in his. His fingers and palm were cool to the touch, making me gasp lightly with the shock against the continued heat of my skin.

"I've not seen you at court before. Has word of my existence truly spread through the court so quickly?" I asked with a chuckle, curling my fingers so that they wrapped around his hand in turn. He pursed his lips as he raised my hand to his mouth, touching his lips to the back of it gently without ever taking his eye contact from me.

"How could people not speak of a beauty like yours?" he asked, that poisonous tongue filled with charm.

I laughed, but the sound was missing any venom I might have otherwise had for a man who thought to bed me by delivering half-truths that lacked any and all passion or significance. While they were clearly true words, else he wouldn't have been able to speak them at all, I felt certain they were the kind he spoke to every woman who crossed his path.

That suited me just fine.

I didn't want a romance that would last a lifetime. I just wanted a passion that would last a night.

"I bet all the girls fall for that line," I said, feeling it necessary to make him aware that I was onto his game. That I did not take him to bed for some naivety he could take advantage of. In this, our relationship could be mutually beneficial, and I could use him just as much as he sought to use me.

"Not all of them," he said, having the decency not to attempt to hide his rakish charm. I smiled, painted red lips spreading over my teeth as I drew my hand back from him slightly. He didn't release it, instead turning with me as I faced the direction that would lead to the stairs and, ultimately, my bedroom.

I would not relegate Pax to her tiny room tonight, hoping there was another place she could go to occupy her time if I gave her the night off. While I was more than comfortable with an audience after all the times I'd fucked in the hot springs buried in the tunnels of the Resistance, I didn't think the shy woman had any interest in knowing what noises I, or Soren, made when deep in the throes of passion.

"I don't need pretty words that we both know serve a single purpose," I said, leaning in to whisper the words as I took the first step. Soren tucked my hand into his arm, following along with my gait as I made my way toward the stairs. "In fact, I don't even want them. I've no desire to belong to any man, let alone a God."

"Then what is it you want, Princess?" Soren asked, those odd silver eyes gleaming as he stared down at me. We moved to the stairs as he released me to allow me to gather up the length of my dress so I could climb the steps without issue. The lights of the chandeliers played off his hair, bringing out the subtle purple notes beneath the near-black color.

"I can think of far better uses for your mouth, Soren," I said, watching as his brow rose in surprise. He huffed a soft laugh, wrapping a hand around my waist and guiding me to the alcove that rested on one of the stairway landings.

I giggled as he tucked me into the wall, leaning his height over me and smiling down at me. "Is that so? I would love to hear what these uses might entail."

He raised his hand to my face, catching my bottom lip with his thumb and tugging it down to reveal my teeth and tongue. "It doesn't involve my mouth," I said, grabbing him by the wrist. I guided his hand down over the front of my throat and through the line of my cleavage, drawing a path over the fabric that covered my stomach.

Lower.

Lower.

"Ahem." A male voice interrupted the moment, and I dropped my head back onto the stone wall in irritation.

I'd been so close to sneaking away.

"A little busy," Soren said, not even bothering to tear his eyes from mine. But I'd already released his hand, pressing my palms flat into the stone behind me

"I see that," Etan said, and his form appeared as he stepped out of the shadows at the top of the stairs, seemingly having taken another stairwell to head us off before we could reach my rooms. "Given that you have your filthy hands all over my soon-to-be wife, I thought it prudent that I interrupt your little seduction."

Soren backed away a few steps, raising his hands as if he were innocent. "I'm not sure who you think is doing the seducing here, but I can assure you it wasn't me," he said with a laugh, throwing me entirely under the carriage to be trampled on by the Summer Court Fae, whose eyes were no longer filled with warmth.

They'd cooled considerably, hardening like molten lava as I rolled my eyes.

"Don't be pathetic. It doesn't suit you," I snarked at Soren, watching as his gaze bounced between me and Etan as he tried to make sense of the situation.

"Is it true? Are you betrothed to marry him?" he asked, raising a brow as if marriage mattered to any of the Fae. It was nothing to them, a business agreement meant to uphold political alliances until a mate bond came and ruined them all anyway.

"It isn't not true," I said, injecting exasperation into every word.

Soren grinned, shaking his head as he backed away. Etan glared at him as he made his way to the stairs that would take him back down to the entryway, and the probability of finding another toy to play with. "Let me know if you two figure out what this is. I'm happy to join in whatever capacity you like."

I quirked a brow, my interest piqued. Glancing at Etan, I found his own features still twisted into a scowl, and him uninterested in the blatant offer of the other man.

Dammit.

That could have been fun.

Soren disappeared down the stairs, leaving me to push off the stone wall and make my way toward my room. Etan filled the space Soren had vacated, pressing his hands at my waist and pushing me back once again. He too towered over me, leaning into my space as he glared down at me. "What the fuck was that?" he asked, and I'd have been lying if I said my gaze didn't wander to the tension in his forearms where he'd rolled up his tunic sleeves.

The muscles bulged there, and the stupid, unrelenting desire to drag my tongue over them was unwelcome.

"A girl has needs, Etan," I snapped, forcing myself to glare. "He was available to tend to them. It's not that serious." I would *not* admit that Etan would have likely been my first choice for a bed partner if he hadn't come with all sorts of complications.

I didn't do those.

"If only you were spoken for and had a man who was capable of meeting those needs for you," he snapped back.

"I'm not interested in that offer. I wanted him because I could forget his name by morning," I said, watching the way Etan's jaw clenched. I was playing with literal fire, his eyes blazing as he pressed his torso into my chest and pinned me into the wall. My words weren't entirely untrue, letting me speak them. I might have been interested in Etan, but this kind of possessiveness was exactly why I would not be interested in his offer.

"Do not tempt me, Sunfire. I swear to fucking Gods, I will cut off his cock and feed it to the Cwn Annwn before I allow him to touch you with it," Etan snarled.

"Well, that would be a waste of a perfectly good cock," I teased, grinning up at him in an attempt to ease some of the tension that didn't serve me.

It didn't work.

"Fallon."

"Oh, first names. I must be in trouble," I said, rolling my eyes. "I don't do complicated, Etan, and you, my lovely soon-to-be husband, are the very definition of complicated. I have to tolerate you beyond fucking you, and at this point in time, I've yet to determine if that's possible, even without knowing how you feel inside me. We do not need to add the layer of sex to this dynamic."

Etan growled, a warning rumbling in his chest as I touched my hands to it and pressed up onto my tippy-toes. The motion put us even closer, my breath wafting over his throat and his lips brushing the tip of my nose. He tilted his head down, putting his mouth so close to mine that I could practically taste him. He slid a hand beneath the curtain of my dark hair, grasping a handful of it and holding me still. "Let me tell you how this is actually going to go, Sunfire," he murmured, trailing his nose over my jaw as he turned my head with his grip on my hair. His lips trailed over the side of my neck, lighting a path on fire as he moved. "I am going to fuck you until no one doubts who owns you, not even you. It is only a matter of time before you beg me for it, and while we wait for you to come to your senses and stop resisting whatever this attraction is between us, just know one hard truth." He pressed the hard length of his cock into my belly as he snipped at my throat.

"What truth is that?" I whispered, my voice failing me.

"I will fucking slaughter anyone you think to play with until you come to me. We are either celibate or we own one another, no other option exists," he said, releasing his hold on my hair and stepping back from me finally. He left me panting there, driven to the point of near madness even though he'd barely touched me.

"You don't fucking own me."

Etan only grinned. "I think you'll find that I do actually, *wife*," he said, shoving his hands into the pockets of his trousers and leaving me to gape at him as he went to join in on whatever festivities had occurred since we'd left.

Motherfucker.

SEVEN

FALLON

Estrella screamed, the sound shattering something within me. I took a step forward to reach her, grimacing as Etan grabbed my forearm with a vise grip that prevented me from moving.

A blade protruded from Caldris's heart, Mab's iron dagger making him sputter and cling to the last vestiges of life. "Let me go!" I screamed, desperate to make my way to Estrella. She needed me, needed the bond that swayed between us as her bond with her mate prepared to sever.

She couldn't be alone if he left this world—couldn't be alone when she followed after him.

"Stay out of the way," Etan murmured, leaning close so that the words hung between us. "I won't let you risk yourself for her. Estrella made her bed with every moment she chose to defy Mab. There is *nothing* you can do to change her fate now," he said, casting his gaze toward his King. Rheaghan lingered at the edge, his mouth tight and hands fisted at his side. As if he wanted to step in to interfere with his sister's violence but knew better than to defy her.

But like so many of us, something in Estrella's pain drew us closer. Something in that *love* made her striking ability to pull us into her orbit even stronger.

Mab pulled back the blade with her good hand as she cradled her injured one as protectively as she could, and I watched in stunned horror as a surge of blood rose to the surface and dribbled down Caldris's chest in tune with the beating of his heart. I pulled at Etan's grip, trying to get free to no avail.

He simply pulled me into his chest, tucking my back against him and holding steady. His arms wrapped around my chest, entrapping me in a cage I had no hope of freeing myself from no matter how I writhed against him. "Settle, Fallon," he said, keeping his breathing slow and even. It was such a contrast to mine, so in opposition to the racing of my heart. My finger throbbed where the teardrop marked Estrella and me as bonded, the need to intervene coursing through me.

Estrella dropped to her knees at Caldris's side, pressing her hands to his wound as he toppled to his side. She caught him, pulling him into her lap as tears splashed down her face.

"There's been a change of plans," Mab said, her voice calm. It was the perfect display of just how little she cared for anything living—anything breathing.

Caldris was her stepson, the son of her husband, and she'd known him since he was a boy. Her cruelty knew no bounds, to only finally kill him when he was so close to being mated, so close to reaching his euphoria.

Mab wiped her knife on the fabric of her dress, staining it with Caldris's blood.

"I love you," Caldris whispered, the words meant only for his mate. I screamed, knowing about the bond Estrella and Caldris had sworn.

Where one went, the other would follow.

"You don't understand," I whimpered, the sound as broken as I felt inside. Etan shushed me quietly, intending to soothe me as it made his chest vibrate at my spine.

I felt like my heart might tear in two, and Etan held me tight as Mab's curious gaze swung toward me. She studied me as if she couldn't comprehend my heartache, as if love were a weakness that made no sense in this instant. I couldn't even blame her, because she didn't yet understand what she'd done.

She didn't understand that she'd ripped Estrella from me. I felt as if I were waiting for a piece of my soul to be torn from my chest, for the inexplicable bond that I felt with Estrella to vanish and take me with it.

She was the only person in this world who could understand. Who knew what it had been like living in Nothrek and belonging in Alfheimr. She may not have known it in her mind, but she'd felt that call coming from the other side of the Veil.

She was the only one capable of offering me the freedom that could only come when Mab was dead. She was my only *hope*.

"Caldris will be the Godly sacrifice. Consider yourself fortunate, Ilaria," she said, the implication of that statement making something in Estrella go blank. Her expression dropped from her face, her anguish vanishing in a moment as she settled inside.

I knew her well enough to know the moment that creature within her rose up to comfort her, wrapping her in an embrace that was so cold that nothing could live within it. This was the Estrella that Mab did not know to fear, the one who made her ramblings about power seem like child's play. The day that Estrella learned to control that part of her would be the day she conquered the world, plunging us into chaos and darkness.

Caldris turned pale, his eyes beginning to glaze over as Estrella's claws extended into talons. She dragged one over her wrist, making a sharp slice across her skin. The scent of blood was metallic in the air, turning my stomach with the strength of it.

"Please don't leave me," she begged, silent tears tracking down her cheeks as she pressed her bleeding wrist to her mate's mouth.

Caldris's eyes drifted closed, and I watched in dawning horror as Estrella's *viniculum* pulsed with shadows. The black seemed to writhe on her skin in agitation, the shadows stretching and twirling as they threatened to consume her. Her eyes were wide, a manic energy I'd never seen on her face. The white of her Fae Mark spread, shimmering with golden light as it shifted and pushed back the dark.

Her blood vanished into Caldris's mouth, the stain of it sparkling with gold where it touched his lips.

"If you are not strong enough to free yourself from this bond that cripples you, then I will do it for you, Little Mouse," Mab said, sneering as Estrella turned her gaze away from her dying mate. The hatred written into the lines of her face promised retribution; it promised violence and vengeance and all the things that would plunge Alfheimr into war. I knew without a doubt that if Estrella lost Caldris, I would lose her. Even before she followed after him in mere moments, her soul would fray in ways that would never be fixed. She would destroy the entire world, burn it all to the ground if it meant tearing Mab's head from her shoulders. Her eyes glowed with golden light, her magic pulsing from within her.

Mab had the intelligence to stagger back half a step, trying to disguise her fear over the monster she'd so foolishly unleashed. Her ownership over Caldris had been the one thing controlling Estrella, had been the one piece that kept her from destruction.

Mab realized her folly as she summoned her daemon to guard her, watching as the creature who could siphon Estrella's magic took up guard beside the Queen who had summoned him from Hel.

Mab's soldiers grabbed Caldris by the legs, attempting to drag his limp form out of Estrella's grip. She held tight with one hand, making them eye her warily as she managed to cling to him. It should have been impossible, the strength she asserted against two men with a single hand to cling to her lost love.

"She's going to kill us all," I said, warning Etan of the coming danger. If Caldris was lost to us, Estrella's rage simmered beneath the surface—ready to explode into the cove with the violence of a thousand storms.

Etan swallowed with a nod, holding my gaze with something far too intimate in his expression. He reached up to cup my cheek, releasing his hold from my chest with that one arm to give me affection in what could very well be our final moments. "No. We'll have plenty of time to fight yet," he said, earning a disgruntled chuckle from me. He would have absolutely no control over Estrella. Her hands fisted at her sides, her fingers twining around the frayed edges of the golden thread of their bond. I couldn't see it, but the phantom magic of it touched my teardrop mark, the feeling pulsing down our bond as she clung to Caldris.

Her brow knit, furrowing to mimic the deep scowl that toyed with her mouth as her nostrils flared. Her head tilted to the side as she watched Mab's growing concern, that promise of violence becoming a deep, slithering thing that we all felt in the cove alongside us, until it was a tangible creature of its own.

Her face relaxed so suddenly my heart stopped, her hand releasing its iron grip on the thread and splaying across Caldris's chest for a brief moment as she felt something I couldn't see. His eyes flung open, the piercing blue of frost lost to the golden light of fate that mirrored Estrella's gaze. Mab gasped, and the daemon swung his sword toward the impending threat.

The *impossible* threat that came with the realization that Estrella had healed a heart stabbed with iron. That she'd kept her mate from the very clutches of the afterlife.

There would be consequences for robbing the Void of the life it was owed, I knew. I knew and didn't care, because it meant that Estrella was whole, that those magical eyes shone with relief.

Estrella realized the intended path of the daemon's blade, as she laid herself over his body, using her own flesh to shield the mate she'd only just saved. I screamed my warning, her name lost to the ringing in my ears as the wind of the daemon's strike moved the hair on Estrella's neck.

No.

Etan tightened his grip as I tried to move to her, to get in the way of the death calling her name this time. I couldn't reach her, couldn't protect her from what I knew would be fatal. . . .

Caldris reached up, his arm moving faster than a lightning strike arcing through the sky. He caught the daemon's blade in his bare hand, stopping it with an explosion of golden light that tore through the cavern and made the tree branches rattle in the woods beside the beach. Sand blew into my face, stinging my eyes as Etan turned me in his grip, shoving my face into his tunic and shielding me as he rounded his body over mine. The sound of something striking the ground was the first to permeate the buzzing haze, like the explosion of light had damaged my ear drums.

I pulled my face out of Etan's chest, blinking up at him with wide, shocked eyes that I suspected mirrored his. His russet-brown gaze roamed over my face, inspecting me for injury in a way I couldn't reconcile. His lips moved, but no sound came as I shook my head at him and reached up a hand to touch my ear.

My fingers came away wet, and I brought them forward to stare down at the blood that trickled down the sides of my neck from whatever damage I'd sustained. The feeling of my body healing itself was one I would never grow used to, the flesh moving within my ears as my body fought to repair the damage caused by Caldris's outburst.

I spun as hearing returned slowly, trickling in through the silence. Caldris had covered Estrella with his body, shielding her from any further harm as he laid her out on top of the sand. She stared up at him in shock, unable to figure out what she'd done to her mate. What she'd made him into by giving him her blood. He did not smile as he inspected her for injury, his face strangely unfeeling as he got to his feet over her. The daemon was nowhere to be found, as if he'd simply vanished into thin air while Etan surrounded me. Estrella scrambled to her feet as the guards charged Caldris, attempting to contain the threat to the Queen they were all forced to serve.

Caldris reached out a hand, his shadows no longer dark. Instead of black tendrils, they glowed with Estrella's golden light as he sent them sweeping toward those who advanced upon them. They wrapped themselves around the guards' throats, squeezing as the other royals stepped back away from the fray. Etan tightened his grip, lifting me off my feet as he too backed away from the spectacle.

"No!" I screamed, thrashing my legs to fight against his grip. I wouldn't leave them to fight this alone, would at the very least bear witness to what my mother did to two of the people I loved more than anything. Estrella was part of me, a part I would never be able to tear from my soul. The crescent moon on my hand that marked us as one and the same seemed to pulse as she glanced up, meeting my stare with a soft smile that spoke of exactly what she knew would happen here. She already knew that she would never walk away from this cove, that there was no possibility in this world that Mab allowed both of them to remain free.

Her face was resigned as she mouthed to me, and I would have sworn I heard her sad voice break through the chaos. "Go," she said, ignoring my head shake to look at Etan and study the way he held me. She pursed her lips, nodding to him with a slight motion that he seemed to recognize as her expectation to protect me.

She would haunt him in the afterlife if he didn't.

Estrella's attention shifted to Mab as she raised a single hand. Her face tipped to the side as Mab held Estrella's stare, watching as the Queen's gaze fell to the already healed wound on Estrella's wrist. The blood that stained her skin shimmered with gold, with the distinct sign of the Primordials that Estrella had fought to keep secret in the face of Mab's suspicion. What she proposed was impossible, and yet . . .

There was no denying what Estrella was capable of.

Caldris finished with the guards, turning his attention to the Queen who had enslaved him as a weapon for all those years. Who had allowed her people to violate him in the greatest way, robbing him of autonomy over his own person.

Mab squeezed her hand as Etan backed me away slowly, attempting to avoid drawing attention to us and our retreat. Caldris grimaced but continued on through the pain, pushing through her control on him even as his chest stilled and stopped heaving with breath. Estrella struggled in turn, her face pinching with agony that I knew existed only in her heart. Their bond was incomplete, his pain only a shadow of what it would be had they been able to accept it. Caldris dropped to his knees, clutching his chest as his eyes flashed back and forth between blue and gold.

"Stop!" Estrella begged, squeezing her eyes closed. She was trapped, desperate to save her mate, and I knew what she would do to save him, knew the sacrifice she would make. I couldn't fault her for it, knowing I would have done nothing less to save *her*. "Name your price."

"My star," Caldris wheezed, reaching toward her with his free hand. He would rather see both of them dead than see her enslaved to Mab as so many others had been, than see his one love turned into a brutal weapon and know the guilt she wouldn't be able to escape for an eternity.

My mother grinned, clearly pleased with the turn of events. This may not have been what she'd intended when she set forth with this task, but she was positively gleeful about it nonetheless. Meanwhile, my heart felt like it was being torn in two, knowing that there was *nothing* I could do to help her without any magic or control over it. My helplessness was a prison all its own, leaving me shaking with the feeling that I might come out of my skin. That something within me wanted to *burn*.

Mab tossed her head back and laughed, the sound filling the cavern. "We both know there is only one thing I want from you, Little Mouse," she said, stepping closer slowly. She only stopped when she stood before Estrella, pressing the tip of the blade into the skin above her heart.

"Estrella, NO!" Caldris screamed, the agony of that yell making the hair on my arms rise.

"Don't do it," a male voice pleaded, drawing my gaze away from Estrella and Mab and the spectacle they made. Rheaghan raised his hands placatingly, as if he could convince his sister that he was no threat to her. Etan winced at my back, stilling in his retreat as his King's gaze collided with his. Rheaghan gave him a look that said not to intervene, that no matter what happened, he was to stay out of it. I felt Etan shake his head at my spine, his grip tightening on me as

Rheaghan's gaze dropped to me for the briefest of moments before he swung his attention back to Estrella. "It cannot be undone. I don't think you understand what an eternity of servitude will mean."

"I consent. As long as he lives," Estrella said, the words torn from the depths of her soul. Caldris's horror was palpable in the air, striking me deep in the chest with an anguish I hoped I would never understand. I didn't want to love anyone that completely, not if it meant feeling pain like that.

Mab wasted no time gliding the edge of her blade along Estrella's skin, cutting through the muscle and sinew to create a gash that leaked blood on her dress in a steady stream. She carefully avoided Estrella's heart itself, unwilling to lose the weapon she'd only just claimed for herself. For any mortal, the wound would have been fatal within seconds.

But Estrella stayed standing, her silence ringing through the cove as she refused to give even a whimper of pain. I didn't know how she did it, how she survived and endured endlessly without ever giving in.

I would have given up long ago.

Mab raised her other arm, the one with the torn hand—a small snake twined around her wrist. It hissed at Estrella as Mab guided it to the hole she'd created in Estrella's chest, iron-teeth flashing as it slithered inside.

Her wound healed over, and Estrella's entire body shuddered as those iron-teeth sank into the flesh of her heart and turned the key to the prison of her body, shackling her in chains that we couldn't see.

"What have you done?" Rheaghan asked, running a hand through his hair.

Estrella turned to face him, her face distinctly devoid of life. There was no emotion in it during the moments that Mab made herself at home in Estrella's skin, only a blank mask of mindless obedience.

Mab's iron blade lashed out so quickly that I thought for a moment she would go back on her word and take Caldris from Estrella after everything. It would be a small mercy in the end, with the knowledge I possessed that Estrella would go with him.

But it was Rheaghan's throat that parted beneath the blade, his blood trickling down the front of it as his mouth dropped open and he choked. He pressed both hands to that line, that unnaturally straight line that marred his fair skin. Blood poured over his hands in a thick, viscous ooze as he looked to Etan.

I didn't dare to look at the man behind me, at the man who had just lost his King. I didn't know the truth of Etan's allegiance, of what he might feel for Rheaghan even as he betrayed him with Mab, but there was no mistaking the anguished gasp that rattled in his chest or the tightness in his body.

There was no denying the outright devastation on his face as Rheaghan bled.

Everything in me stilled and then rattled, vibrating with fury for the opportunity she'd taken. I'd thought we'd have time to get to know one another outside her watchful gaze. I'd been so sure we would have that opportunity.

I'd been so sure the man at my spine was Mab's ally and my enemy, so determined to keep him at a distance because of it. But he'd been the first one my uncle looked to in his last moments.

He'd been the friendly face he sought out.

Rheaghan fell to his knees at Estrella's side, and Estrella reached out to take his hand in his final moments as *emotion* flooded her once again. Her face was no longer a carefully controlled mask, but one of anguish.

I hadn't realized she'd known Rheaghan that well, hadn't seen them together but a handful of times, but there was no mistaking her grief as Mab drove her knife into his heart, silencing him permanently. Estrella moved as if she might give him her blood, and I knew she intended to save the King of the Summer Court, even though she'd already greatly weakened herself. She had *nothing* left to give.

Mab abandoned her blade to squeeze her hand, forcing Estrella to halt and preventing her from interfering. Estrella fought against it, against that hold on her as her body refused to move. Rheaghan bled out before us, and none so much as dared to attempt to save him.

It wasn't his sister he looked to in his final moments, nor was it Etan as his second-in-command. He looked to Estrella as he died, as if he saw her for the first time, and his eyes filled with sorrow.

He dropped onto the sand face-first, bleeding out upon the white silt. There was no movement in his chest, not a breath in his body.

Because the King of Summer was dead.

Eight

ETAN

I stared at the space that Rheaghan had once occupied, his body nothing more than flesh on the sand. I knew he was gone, but I couldn't quite bring myself to grasp the reality of a world without him in it.

He'd been there for every moment of my life, an echo of my own heartbeat that came from the type of friendship that spanned lifetimes. Only Fallon held within my grip kept me from surging toward him, from revealing just how much I still respected Rheaghan.

Revealing everything we'd worked so hard to keep hidden from Mab would only attract attention that would get us both killed, because Mab would not tolerate the knowledge that I'd been loyal to anyone but her—not when her hatred for the way her brother was loved was a deep, festering wound that she could never heal.

Caldris raced for his mate, anguish and relief mixing on his face when he was able to draw her into his arms. I couldn't help the bitterness I felt, knowing that if Estrella had only been willing to let Caldris go, Rheaghan would still walk the land of the living.

I wouldn't need to keep the surge of emotions hidden behind a carefully controlled mask—always holding steady to the role that Rheaghan had given me so long ago.

Instead, I watched a daemon emerge from the tree line to grasp him by the ankles, hauling him into the cove as Mab stared passively at the brother that had once meant so much to her. He'd been her protector as a child, the two of us doing everything in our power to keep her safe from those who would use her to get to her mother. But the Mab of this day didn't seem to care that she'd killed him. She didn't care that Rheaghan had *loved* being her brother as a child, taken to that role as if he'd been born for it.

She'd never deserved it. Not since the moment that crown touched her head and claimed her for cruelty. Now more than ever, I knew there was nothing worth redeeming left in the woman who stood before me.

Even after all this time, Rheaghan had loved the memory of his sister enough that he hadn't been able to rise up against her. In the face of that loyalty, she'd cared only for his insolence, her jealousy, and the challenge he presented to her.

Of all the things Mab had done, of all the people she'd killed, ending the life of the one person who still believed in her was the worst. It meant that when all was said and done and I finally left the Shadow Court again, I would do so not only grieving my best friend but also grieving the end of the very thing he'd sacrificed his life for.

His death was for nothing. His *life* had been for nothing—protecting a woman who was beyond salvation.

A woman I had every intention of watching die when the time came.

"You're mine now," Mab said, snapping out a hand to catch Estrella by the chin. She screamed as Mab's talons cut into her skin, but from what I knew of the young woman, it wasn't the physical pain that brought her to yell.

It was the will pressing down on her soul.

"I have need of something that is locked within Tartarus," Mab said, clicking her tongue as she turned to look at the shimmering cove. It looked innocent enough, a perfect disguise for the horrors locked within.

"No," Caldris rasped. Most who went to Tartarus were changed forever, their souls irrevocably damaged. The few who returned at all often begged for death.

"Bring me a snake from the crown of Medusa," Mab ordered, nodding toward that shimmering pool. Estrella moved to obey, her legs shifting even as she grimaced. Mab gestured to one of her guards, and the male moved to give Estrella the clasped scabbard from his waist. He ignored Caldris's growl as he touched Estrella to settle it at her waist. It was far too large for her, and I knew that whatever she had to fight, it would be too heavy to be of practical use for her. No amount of Fae-like strength could accommodate the way it would interfere with her balance.

Still, I didn't move to intervene. The only thoughts in my head were for Fallon and my people.

My people, in the absence of Rheaghan.

Horror came swiftly, the dawning realization that Mab's decision to end her brother's life came so quickly on the heel of the choice to wed her daughter to me. I'd planted that seed in her mind, not with the intention of ever ruling the Summer Court, but that didn't change the reality of the situation.

Mab had made her daughter the rightful Queen by murdering her own brother.

Imelda hurried forward, bypassing where I stood with Fallon. The two women exchanged a panicked gaze, Fallon fighting against my hold even as I shifted her to the side and stared down at all the blood that had been spilled. All the blood that belonged to Rheaghan, that should have been contained within the confines of his body. Imelda pressed a small pouch into Estrella's hands, but the grief-stricken expression on the witch's face said that she knew exactly how useless it would be to Estrella. Without Imelda's guidance, the young Fae wouldn't have the slightest clue what to do with whatever herbs or poultices she'd given her.

Estrella's mouth pressed into a tight line as she nodded anyway, accepting the aid that she could only hope to decipher. I suspected the intention behind the gift meant more to her than what the satchel may actually contain. From what I'd learned of Estrella in her time at Tar Mesa, she'd moved through her life feeling largely alone. She'd had a mother and brother in her village, but everyone she loved, every moment of happiness she ever managed to find, continued to be torn away from her. This was no different, the support system she'd found in Fallon and Imelda taken from her. Her bond with

Caldris nearly severed by his near death, and now her physical form being sent away from him and into the pits of Tartarus.

She had people who loved her, but she would yet again have to fight her battles alone, without anyone to stand beside her.

I understood her better than I cared to admit, grasped the concept of being alone in a crowded room better than most. I knew what it was to stand apart from all those you considered allies and friends, to be distinctly different in a way that could never be altered. I would never stand beside the likes of Rheaghan and Mab and belong, even though we'd all been raised together. I would never belong in Mab's court along with her cronies, nor would I wholly belong in the Summer Court where I'd been raised, sitting upon the throne Mab intended to keep for me, if my marriage to her daughter was any indication.

I was no God, and I already felt the weight of each and every God who did not have a court to claim as his or her own upon my face. I felt the danger in that stare, the competition lurking should Mab's loyalty falter for even the briefest of moments. Estrella may have prepared to descend into a place of untold danger, but there was no safety to be found above the surface either.

Fallon's tears dripped off her cheek as Estrella took a step toward the cove, her weighted gaze heavy on her mate's. He stepped alongside her, refusing to release the hand he'd claimed with his. He would go anywhere with her, do anything for her. As the other part of his soul, he had little choice but to do everything in his power to protect his other half. While others of my kind coveted that bond, wanted nothing more than to find their other half and move into their destiny with them at their side, I did not envy those who found it. I wanted no part in a mate bond, hoping that my time to pass into the Void would come before I ever found the other half who would weaken me so greatly.

To love was to be vulnerable. To love was to be controlled.

I did not wish to ever give anyone that sort of power over me, not when I knew the damage it could cause. My relationship with Fallon would be different. It could be the ease of friendship and companionship while meeting one another's needs.

Mutually beneficial, but lacking the soul-crushing heartache when it eventually ended. All we had to do was be smart about it and guard our hearts from one another.

After watching so many hearts be stolen by Mab over the years, I'd become very gifted at keeping mine for myself.

One of Mab's men stepped forward to grab Caldris around the back of the neck, tossing him onto the sand. Estrella spun, her eyes wide with fear that Mab would somehow go back on her word. That Caldris would not be safe, that all of this would be for nothing and she'd find him dead when she returned.

Fallon kicked with so much force that I nearly stumbled, shocked by the vehemence in her motions. "Let go!" she shrieked, the realization that Estrella would traverse this journey alone pushing her fight into overdrive.

I forced her backward, dragging her toward the entrance to the cove as she fought against me. Holding on to her was like attempting to tame a wild animal, like caging a wildcat that wanted nothing more than to tear the skin from my limbs and feast on my flesh. "She'll be alright," I murmured, the gentleness of my voice so at odds with the violence of her screams. They echoed off the chamber walls as I guided her back into the narrow passageway that would take us to the palace of Tar Mesa, leaving the cove entirely. I couldn't trust Fallon not to follow after Estrella, couldn't have any faith that my future wife would have the sense to save herself.

We emerged into Tar Mesa, the Sidhe and Lliadhe who hadn't been permitted to join the Tithe staring at us as we passed.

"You can't know that!" Fallon shrieked, dropping all her weight to the ground suddenly. I grunted, leaning forward to scoop her off the floor and fling her over my shoulder. The breath expelled from her lungs the moment her stomach connected with my shoulder, offering a brief reprieve from her sounds of rage before she caught her breath. "Put me down, you asshole!"

I'd grown fond of the idea of a wife, developed a fondness for the woman I'd gotten to know in secret. While our marriage might have been an arrangement in her mind, it wasn't one that I could see myself entering into with anyone else. Fallon was impossible and infuriating, her unwillingness to do what it took to keep herself safe something that would undoubtedly cause me untold aggravation in our future together.

But she was also one of the most loyal Fae I'd ever met; the very thing that would create problems for me was the exact thing I craved for myself. I may not have been capable of loving her, but that didn't mean I didn't desire to know her love for myself.

It was wrong, terrible even, for me to expect something of her that I would never be able to offer her in return.

Yet, as Caldris's roar shook the walls around us, I resolved myself to the notion of never loving the woman I would soon marry.

I would never feel that pain.

Nine

FALLON

Every step jostled my body on Etan's shoulder, leaving me more and more aggravated. I hated the feeling of pressure in my ribs, and I was filled with the urge to drive my own shoulder into his stomach when he finally had to release me.

The bastard couldn't carry me forever.

Caldris's pained bellow left me with no choice but to accept that Estrella was gone, that Mab had succeeded in tearing them apart. There was no other reason that an agony like that could exist; only the loss of a mate or a child was worth the pain in that sound. I wished there was something I could do to ease his pain, that I could take Estrella's place in Tartarus. I'd thought I was doing the right thing in allowing her to show Mab her power, in sacrificing myself to a loveless marriage so that Estrella would not need to know the pain of separation from Caldris.

Only for a far worse fate to befall them in spite of my best intentions.

"This is your fault," I groaned, settling on Etan's shoulder for a brief moment. Letting him believe I'd given up the fight, I resolved to show him a quiet complacency that would disarm him. But I would try to follow after her when he was unsuspecting.

And if I couldn't do that?

I'd punish him *for* the fact that he had robbed me of my only chance to intervene. He'd stripped away the minimal chance I had, and I would make sure he suffered for it.

"How am I responsible for Mab's actions?" he asked, his voice incredulous. As if he couldn't believe I would dare to fault him for what she'd done. Even though I knew I couldn't, I could fault him for keeping me from helping her.

"You're responsible for keeping me away from her! I can go with her and help!" I protested, searching for something to grab onto that would *hurt*. Godsdamn the man, but there wasn't an inch of excess skin to spare. My hands roamed over his spine and the sides of his back, looking for any sign of a love handle that I could dig my nails into and try to tear from his body.

Even I was surprised by the venom I felt for him, the wish that he would simply disappear from my life, when he was just as much stuck with me as I had been with him. I glanced down at the swell of his ass, swallowing as I realized I wasn't quite *that* desperate to hurt him. Putting my hands on any part of my future husband that could be seen as *intimate* hardly seemed in my best interest when I had every intention of keeping this arrangement celibate.

"And what do you think that would have accomplished?" he asked, grasping the handle on a door that was very much *not* mine. I didn't recognize this part of the palace, this hallway somehow brighter than the one Mab had given me rooms in for the proximity to hers. There were more candelabras along the stone wall, the warmth of the yellow-and-orange hues of candlelight playing off the coolness of the hall in a way that made my skin warm.

The room inside was smaller than my own, but a huge bay window overlooked the sand-filled terrain outside. The moons shone in through the window, illuminating the room with a glow that felt bright against my eyes as they fought to adjust to the sudden light. I'd spent most of my life locked in the darkness of the tunnels the rebellion called home, only to be trapped in the Court of Shadows almost the moment I stepped foot in Alfheimr. The moments I'd spent in the sun were far too few, but I would take the feeling of moonlight on my skin in its wake. A daybed was nestled into the bay window, as if the person who had furnished this room wanted to be as close to any light source as possible.

Etan approached it after he kicked the bedroom door closed behind him, and the motion tore me away from the moonlight in a way that made my stomach clench. I didn't want to be plunged into darkness again, and his broad, maddening form shielded me from the light as he put distance between us and the door. He drew me over his shoulder so quickly I gasped, dropping me onto the daybed unceremoniously.

I landed with an "oomph," throw pillows bouncing above my head. One fell on my face, and I shoved it to the side as I sputtered and stared up at the Fae male. He stared down at me, his head tilting to the side as his lips parted, as if he couldn't quite figure me out. The retort I'd been about to admonish him with died in my throat, leaving me to swallow the words in discomfort. Something in that look made me want to curl up in a ball, to hide myself from his view entirely.

He reached down, touching a single fingertip to the fair skin of my arm where the moonlight shone against it. His smile was sad and hollowed out as he stared at the place where he touched me. It took away a moment of my anger, showing me a glimpse of the man who appeared to be grieving his own loss, the same as I was.

"You're beautiful even in darkness, but in the light. . . ." He trailed off, shaking his head as if he could clear such thoughts from his mind. I didn't know what to make of the odd sort-of compliment, the unfinished thought hanging between us as I pursed my lips.

"Why am I here?" I asked, pushing up onto my elbows. He blocked me from the door, his broad, hulking form preventing my escape.

I didn't want to take the time to think of all the solid muscle I'd felt beneath his tunic when I'd tried to find a way to hurt him, to contemplate how long it had been since I'd felt the flesh of another against mine. I watched his mask slide into place, all traces of grief fleeing from his expression. If I hadn't been watching him so closely, I would never have believed just how efficiently he slipped into the role he seemed determined to play.

But there were traces of something more in him, hints of a man that I didn't understand at all. If he loved Rheaghan enough to make that mask falter, then why was he loyal to Mab?

"You were too busy groping me to answer my question. What do you think you would have accomplished by going into Tartarus with her?" he asked, and while the tone he used was harsh, there was a teasing tilt to his mouth that I wanted to slap off his face.

This version of Etan was brash and arrogant, and I hated that I had to wonder which version of him was actually real.

"I wasn't groping you! I was looking for a way to *maim* you," I snapped, my mouth dropping open in shock as heat flooded my cheeks. The burn in them gave me away, hinted at the fact that I hadn't particularly *not* enjoyed my search, much to my dismay.

"Whatever you want to call it. You can *maim* me whenever you like, Sunfire," he said, taking a step back just when I thought he might reach for me.

My lungs filled with air suddenly as I took my first full breath. His presence was so imposing, so shocking to my system, that I felt like my body forgot how to function around him. I wasn't myself, and I couldn't even claim he made me into the best version of myself.

I felt certain he made me into the worst possible version with only his nearness. If he were to ever touch me, I felt as if I might burst into the fires of Hel itself and burn him with me out of petty spite. His gaze softened as he studied me, and he reached out a hand to take mine as he leaned down toward me. "We have to get out of Tar Mesa. I'm going to ask Mab for permission to leave for the Summer Court. It isn't safe here now. You don't know Mab like I do; there will be consequences for all of us. She'll grieve what she's done in her own way, and that will involve a downward spiral of more death and suffering."

I snapped my hand back, blinking up at him in shock. "I'm not leaving Estrella to rot in the cove and Imelda to suffer here without me! You cannot ask that of me."

"Then you leave me no choice," he sighed, turning on his heel and making his way to the door. I scrambled to the edge of the daybed as he grasped the handle, turning it and pulling it open without so much as a glance back at me. "Wait!" I shouted, tripping over my own legs as I scrambled to my feet. He stepped out of the room hurriedly, pulling the door closed behind him as I struggled. There was the distinctive sound of a key turning in the lock, and by the time I reached the door, it was too late. I tried the knob anyway, twisting it with both hands frantically before I slammed my palm against the chestnut wood. "What are you doing?!"

"Since you clearly cannot be trusted to prioritize your own self-preservation, I will do it for you. I am not foolish enough to believe you do not have every intention of following Estrella into Tartarus," he said. His voice was eerily calm on the other side, a distinctive decidedness to his tone that brooked no argument.

"You overstep your place, Etan!" I yelled, banging a fist against the door. The wood rattled but didn't so much as creak as my knuckles throbbed. A reminder that I was barely a step from human, a *powerless* Sidhe that could do nothing to help herself in the games of the Fae.

"Do I?" he asked with a chuckle, and even though I couldn't see him, I could just imagine him leaning his shoulder into the door that served as a barrier between us. "You're new to our ways, so I will grant you the kindness of explaining what is going to happen now." I swallowed, pressing my back into the door in response. I hung on every word, waiting as if his voice were the blade prepared to perform my execution. "You became mine the moment your mother and I agreed to this betrothal. In such, she acknowledged that you are seemingly powerless, and until such a time when you come into your own magic, you and your safety are my responsibility as your husband. You may not understand what a queen will mean to our people after centuries without one, but I do, and I have no intention of seeing them robbed of that before they ever even lay eyes upon you."

My voice shook when I finally responded, swallowing down the panic rising in my throat as I stared at the moons shining in the night sky. My eyes watered at the prospect of moving into just another cage, that in spite of Mab's words that Etan wouldn't hurt me, she didn't acknowledge that there was more than just physical pain. "That can't be true. Most courts are ruled by equals—why would that not be true of us?"

His voice dropped lower, a near-silent command that shattered any illusions I might have had regarding the type of marriage we might have. "I have no doubt that one day, we will be equals. But until I can trust you not to throw your life away, I will do whatever I have to do to protect you from yourself. Even if that means taking away your freedom to do it."

Ten

ETAN

I made my way through the halls, unable to bring myself to regret the harsh words I'd given Fallon. While they may not have been fun for her to hear and might have made her regret the future that we would have together, she needed to know that when I said I would do whatever it took to keep her safe, I meant it. I would act against her wishes if it meant looking out for her in the way she seemed unwilling to do for herself. I would lock her in a room to prevent her from putting herself in harm's way.

And I would conspire to sneak her out of Tar Mesa while her only friends and allies slept, making it impossible for them to try to stop me from removing her from the growing threat of her mother.

A woman who was capable of murdering her brother, the man who had been closer to her than any other I could recall, would not hesitate to murder the daughter she considered a great disappointment. In all my experience with Mab, once someone was out of her sight, they were typically out of mind. She didn't spare time to think of those she could not reach to harm, and taking Fallon to the Summer Court was undoubtedly in her best interest—even if she vehemently disagreed with the sentiment.

I knew where I would find Mab without asking any of the courtiers I passed, their pale faces a good indication of the horror they'd witnessed. None had been present for the Tithe; very few were permitted outside of those who had the magic of the Gods in their veins. Only Mab's chosen favorites were allowed, unless they were an active part of the Tithe, and the common Sidhe who roamed the hall were not on her list of special pets.

I descended the stairs toward the entrance, curving my way toward the throne room and the screams that came from within. A male Sidhe stepped out of the shadows, his face drawn. "Terence," I said, nodding to him as I closed the distance between us. Inside the throne room, the woman's screams reached a new level, the sound of her pain echoing off the stone walls. I shoved my reaction to it down, forcing my face to remain an indifferent mask as I met the Summer Court Fae's gaze.

"What do we do now?" he asked, blinking his dark eyes as he seemed to attempt to shake off the stupor that Rheaghan's death had left us all in. He'd been our King for so long, it seemed impossible to know how to move forward without him to guide us.

I clapped my hand down on the male's shoulder, holding his stare as his nostrils flared. Some of the pallor faded from his deep brown skin, his breath evening out as we stood there. In spite of the horror being committed, we would make a plan between us to guide the rest of our people who had come to the Shadow Court along with us. The ones who may not have heard the news of Rheaghan's death yet. "Gather the others. Tell them to pack quickly. We leave tonight," I said, earning his wide eyes.

"Will she allow that?" he asked, swallowing as he glanced through the entryway.

"She will if she wants her daughter to be queen," I said, smiling slightly. His mouth pressed into a line, his disapproval of my pending marriage very clear in the drawn lines of his face. No one would approve of Fallon until they knew her, because unknowns were not welcome in Alfheimr. I'd known I would face an uphill battle in endearing her to my people when we returned home, as all any of us knew about her was that she was the daughter of the Queen of Air and Darkness herself. There was no reassurance that she would be a kind queen when all that my people knew of her was her lineage, and it would take time to reframe her from Mab's daughter to Rheaghan's niece.

That was not an easy hurdle to overcome, I admitted. I'd thought I would have time to conquer that without the pressures of a crown weighing us down. She could make the people adore her while she maintained an irrelevant position as the wife to Rheaghan's second-in-command, something that few would concern themselves over.

"This was her plan all along, wasn't it?" he asked, his voice going soft. "The moment she betrothed her daughter to you, she had already decided to kill Rheaghan."

"I don't know," I admitted, shaking off the guilt that clung to my chest. I'd been the one to put the idea in her head of Fallon and I marrying, and if that was true, I didn't want to think of the fact that I'd also inadvertently made her decide she would rather see her daughter on the throne than her brother. The guilt of that would swallow me whole, and even as an unknown, it was something that would be with me for the rest of my life. "It doesn't matter much now. All we can do is stress that Fallon and I need to return home to be crowned before one of the Gods decides to try to take advantage of an unruled court. Make sure our people are ready quickly."

I moved into the open doorway to the throne room, not bothering to spare a glance for the woman who knelt on the stone floor before the dais. I didn't know her name, didn't *want* to know it. It was far easier to sleep at night when the victims were faceless, when they didn't have names to accompany their screams. "My Queen," I said, kneeling to the side of the dais. I knew better than to get between Mab and her latest plaything, instead choosing to hang my head forward in complete subjugation and wait for her to acknowledge me.

She withdrew her shadows from the woman, and I saw the woman's quivering mass fall to her stomach on the floor. I still refused to look at Mab, keeping my eyes pinned to the stone. "Etan," Mab said, her steps echoing as she made her way toward me. She descended the stairs slowly, the click of her heeled shoes deliberately paced until the pointed toes of them came into view. "Have you come to scold me, too?" she asked, her voice laced with honey and warning, with seduction and menace.

"Of course not, my Queen," I said, shaking my head. It made me sick to my stomach, but I sank into that well-practiced space where Rheaghan had often sent me to *handle* Mab when she'd been difficult as a girl. To give her the approval she wanted in veiled comments, to lend her my support, all the while attempting to guide her to more... kind decisions in the future. "I am certain you did only what you felt you must."

"He asked me for permission to marry!" she said, stepping away from me. I raised my gaze from the floor, staring up at her in surprise as she spun in an aggravated circle. "Do you know who tempted him to do such a thing?"

"I do not," I said, swallowing back the feelings of betrayal that surged within me. He'd spoken nothing to me, given me no signs that he'd found someone he wanted for more than even just a single night. "He mentioned nothing to me, but then he knew my loyalty lies with you. If he wanted it to remain a secret, I do not believe he would have spoken of it to me."

"He said I would not have noticed her absence, so it is highly unlikely she would have been worthy of his hand at any rate," Mab said, as if she found the thought of her brother marrying beneath his station particularly distasteful. "I offered to find him a suitable bride. He *declined*. Do you believe that?" She waved her injured hand, wrapped in fabric to disguise the truth of what I'd only seen hints of beneath. Even still, the misshapen bulk of it curled in unnaturally, like the bones had never set properly when it healed.

I wondered if this occurred before or after Mab had betrothed Fallon to me. It couldn't have been Fallon herself that she planned to wed to Rheaghan, but I also couldn't put it past Mab entirely. A marriage of convenience didn't need to be consummated, and it would be the easiest way to see her daughter on the throne without giving up her own.

"Perhaps whoever this person is, Rheaghan wanted to marry them because he loved them," I explained, watching as Mab's eyes narrowed in disgust.

"Love," she spat, making her thoughts on the emotion clear. She wanted nothing to do with anything that might weaken her, and that was entirely how she saw the emotion. I couldn't fault her for it, not after having seen the way she used loved ones against her enemies.

"On that, we agree, my Queen," I said, forcing myself to smile up at her. She returned the sentiment, lowering into her throne and raising her good hand to signify that I should stand.

"If I were inclined, I just may have taken you for my own husband, Etan. You are one of my most loyal charges," she said, running her nails over the bare skin of her chest. She'd mentioned it several times, particularly when we'd been children, to the point that I worried she would follow through one day. That I'd be forced to marry a woman I had once seen as a sister, and now only saw as a monstrous damnation of everything she had been once upon a time. But it had never come to pass, not even after she'd rid herself of the husband who gave her the Shadow Court.

She would never again share her throne.

"You honor me, my Queen," I said, the words feeling like ash in my mouth.

"How is my daughter faring, after the loss of her *friend*," she said, the word feeling like an insult. I had no doubt sending Estrella to Tartarus was only partially because the woman seemed more likely to succeed in the quest that Mab's other victims had been unable to do. It also served the purpose of severing her daughter's bond with the woman Fallon valued far more than she ever would her own mother. Stealing Fallon away would mean she was separated from Imelda as well.

I had no doubt that if we remained, Imelda would be the next to suffer Mab's wrath. The thought alone had me glancing toward the figure before the dais, but the woman was a far cry from the witch who'd raised Fallon.

"I detained her in my rooms for the time being," I said, shrugging as if it was inconsequential. "The girl doesn't seem to know how to contain her emotions appropriately, but we will work on that," I said, earning a nod of approval from Mab.

"Good. She could do with a lesson in respect," Mab said, smiling broadly. In the days after my betrothal to Fallon, she'd asserted her expectations that I would bring her wayward daughter to heel. That I would use whatever means I felt were necessary to train Fallon into something Mab could be proud of.

"I apologize to admit that I came to ask a favor of you, my Queen," I said, bowing my head forward. Asking anything of her could be volatile at best, deadly most days.

"You wish to take my daughter and leave," she said, knowing the question I would ask before I could even voice it. It was the strategic move, returning home to fill the void of power. Even Mab had to see that.

"I worry what would happen if one of the other Gods were to return to the Summer Court before Fallon and I have had ample time to make our journey according to our bridal traditions. If her magic truly does belong to the Summer Court, it may not pass to her until she sets foot on summer soil and exposes herself to it. I would hate for it to pass her over in favor of another," I explained, trailing off.

Mab was familiar with the Summer Court and the ways we prepared our brides for marriage, of what occurred in the days leading up to the crowning of a new King and Queen. There was a process to become the heir.

"Fuck the traditions," she said with a scoff, rolling her eyes. "Simply kill anyone who may oppose your rule. It is only a matter of time before Rheaghan's magic passes to Fallon at any rate, and none will be able to argue with her right to rule once that occurs."

"*If* it passes to her. The magic of the Summer Court could always pass to you, my Queen," I said, offering up the uncertainty in who the court itself would choose as heir. There was always a slight unpredictability to it, if the next natural choice was unworthy of such things for any reason. The magic of Faerie was wild and untamed and often did whatever it wanted; lineage was a strong indicator, but not the ultimate one.

"No, I've long since given up hope that would occur. If I thought it possible, I'd have killed Rheaghan sooner. The magic of the Summer Court will pass over me. The light has long been lost to me in a way that will never recover," she said, staring off into the distance for a moment. There was something almost wistful about her expression, an indication that maybe she missed the warmth of her home court.

"Whatever happens, as helpful as it may be to have in the face of opposition, I think it more prudent that we attempt to quell any rebellion before it begins. Fallon honoring traditions that are not her own would go a long way toward endearing her to my people," I said, keeping my voice soft. There was no reproach, only a gentle reminder that a peaceful coup always offered more strength than a violent one.

"Very well, then," Mab said, raising her hand to peel dried blood from her fingers. "I will see that the Gods are not permitted to leave for five days' time. Will that give you the head start you require to be crowned before any other Gods can make an offering to the magic?" she asked, her stare already turning bored. Her attention on me flagged, moving back to the woman she clearly intended to torment more after I left her in peace.

"That would be most generous of you," I said, nodding my head in agreement.

"Yes, it would, wouldn't it? Off you go, then," she said, her voice eerily cheerful. I swallowed down my unease for the woman she looked to, knowing that she would never leave this throne room alive.

"Thank you, my Queen," I said, turning to give Mab my back and leaving her to her fate as I escaped with those who mattered to me.

"Oh, and Etan?" she called as she descended the steps. The click of her heels forced me to look at her over my shoulder, at the slowly gathering mass of shadows at her side that I prayed were not intended for me. "I expect my daughter to be reformed, next I see her. I would hate to be disappointed in how you handle her."

"Understood," I said, bowing my head before I retreated from the room to the sound of a whip cracking through the air.

But it wasn't meant for me, not yet anyway.

Eleven

ETAN

I bypassed my room, striding straight down the hallway to another that was near enough to mine. While Eryx normally called the Autumn Court home, he'd spent a great many weeks visiting with a lover in the Summer Court a few years prior. In that time, we'd gotten to know him well enough that I felt comfortable asking this favor of him.

Fallon would probably gut him the next time she saw him, but that was something for him to worry about another day.

I knocked on the wooden door, the distinct scent of a warm summer day clinging to the space beyond. It smelled like home, like afternoon naps in the shadow of a tree to escape the sun.

Eryx tugged open the door, stretching with a yawn as he took in my presence. He stepped to the side, allowing me to enter the room that was his haven. Every corner of his space was filled with nooks suited to sleeping, books strewn about as if he only read a few pages before tumbling into slumber. The folded corners of pages made something within me twitch.

"Have you never heard of a bookmark?" I asked, picking a book up off the floor where he'd arranged pillows in front of the windows that overlooked the sandy terrain outside.

"Did you wake me simply to insult my book preferences, or did you need something, Highness?" Eryx said, giving a mocking bow that was in poor taste, considering it had been scarcely an hour since Rheaghan's death.

A growl rumbled in my throat, a warning that I would not tolerate his disrespect.

"Apologies, even I know that was horrible," he admitted, moving to an end table and gathering the wineglass that I suspected could hold enough to put him to sleep for hours. He drew a deep drink, and I sighed with the knowledge that this was how the man coped. He drowned his sorrows in drink and slept until the world seemed brighter. "What is it you need, Etan?" he asked finally, setting the glass down gently.

His hands shook as he moved away from the wine, a slight tremor that hinted at just how deeply the loss of the Summer King had affected him.

How deeply it had affected all of us.

Rheaghan may have been an unabashed rake and frivolous with his choice of lovers, but he was also one of the most fair rulers Alfheimr had ever seen. He didn't discriminate against any in his court, showing no preference for those who were closest to him simply due to their proximity.

In fact, he was far more likely to lay into me when I made a mistake than he was a stranger, offering kind redirection to those he didn't know well.

He was Mab's opposite in every way, and the world would be worse for his loss.

I swallowed down my own grief, focusing on the task at hand. It was what he would expect of me, what he would demand if he'd had the opportunity to instruct me before Mab sent him to an early grave. He would put his people first always, and I needed to do the same to ensure they were cared for in his absence.

"It's time for me and mine to return home. Mab has already given her permission for us to leave," I said, watching as his brows rose in surprise. He'd likely assumed, as I suspected so many did, that we would continue to be held captive in the Shadow Court until Mab tired of toying with us, until the courts could no longer continue to function without the people who led them.

"I'm surprised she did not ask you to stay and offer her comfort after Rheaghan's death," Eryx said, but he nodded as he processed the thought. "What does any of that have to do with me?"

"I'm to marry Mab's daughter, Princess Fallon, so it is of the utmost urgency that she and I return home to claim the Summer Court throne," I explained, answering the question he hadn't actually asked. It was relevant to lead into the one he had voiced, information that would explain why I needed his assistance.

"Congratulations?" he said, but his voice rose at the end with a question. Arranged marriages were usually entered into between two parties who had an equal stake in property or titles, and I supposed Fallon and I did in a way.

She was the last remaining member of her bloodline, the last heir to her grandmother's magic. The Primordial of Light had passed her abilities to both her children, but when Mab had become twisted by the cursed gem upon her crown, she'd lost any and all ability to channel the magic that would associate her with summer. The magic of her brother, the God of the Sun, was lost to her entirely, leaving her far more at home with the Shadow Court, which she would never abandon. Fallon was the only choice to honor the Primordial who had claimed the Summer Court for herself once upon a time, but her magic had yet to manifest.

My own magic was far more at home in the oceans surrounding our court, in the seawater potions my mother had so greatly favored. It was not the magic that any of us had ever seen as being enough to rule, and I could only hope that my court's loyalty to me would be enough. That my years of service at Rheaghan's side would allow them to entrust me with their future. The uncertainty of someone else was too great to bear.

"From what I've seen, Fallon is far more like her uncle than her mother," I said, the statement the greatest compliment I could give. She was fiery and stubborn, but she held the same spark that I'd watched burn in Rheaghan's spirit for years, for centuries even, as he waited for someone to save the sister he had once known from the curse that was hers to bear. "Including the more resistant instincts he possessed."

"She doesn't want to marry you," Eryx said, crossing his arms over his chest as if the turn of events pleased him greatly. "The mighty Etan has finally found a partner who does not desire him, and it's the one he is destined to spend his life beside!"

"I am glad you find it entertaining that I shall need to guard myself even in sleep," I said, unable to resist the urge to smile at the guffaw he released. "But *that* is precisely why I require your assistance. Fallon will not want to leave without the witch who raised her, and we need to make this journey on our own according to tradition. The odds of me sneaking her out of Tar Mesa while she screams are fairly limited, so I would prefer to do it while she sleeps, until we've put some distance between us and those she would choose to lean on when she should be learning to lean on me instead."

"What difference does it make if she learns to rely on you?" Eryx asked, that knowing stare of his probing into mine. His eyes were the palest of blues, and in certain lights, one could even convince themselves they were an opaque white against the gold of his skin, which so thoroughly mimicked the sleep dust he reached into his pocket to grasp a handful of. "Your marriage would typically mean living entirely separate lives outside of court functions."

"She'll be alone in the Summer Court. She's already endured so much change, I feel it is appropriate that she have someone she can trust to turn to—"

Eryx grinned, allowing his dust to slip through his fingers to the floor below. "You *like* her," he said, his laughter echoing the words.

"Don't be ridiculous. I am merely doing what is necessary to make the best of the situation we have found ourselves in. I cannot leave her to wallow in pity when she is my responsibility now," I said, keeping my face carefully blank. While I trusted Eryx under most circumstances, he would not have been able to lie if Mab asked him the right question. Something in Eryx's magic already allowed him to see straight into a person's desires, their wishes and dreams for the future. It had to be the tenuous line that existed between the dreams of sleep and waking, the way our real-world interests influenced the dreamscape we created when there was no one to judge.

No one but Eryx, should he turn his inner eye toward us anyway.

"How fortuitous that Mab selected a wife you will enjoy," Eryx said, each word laced with suspicion. Most thought him to be a quiet God, far more interested in toying with the Sidhe as they slept, but I'd seen him plant the seeds of doubt into a person while they dreamt. I'd seen him guide a person's waking actions by poking around in their dreamscape, the slow manipulation having been largely the inspiration for the way I handled Mab.

It was always the quiet ones who slid through life unnoticed who were capable of the greatest damage.

He was more like me than most of the others in this Godsforsaken court, who acted first with little thought to the long game.

"Are you accusing me of something, Eryx?" I asked, tipping my head to the side. My fingers itched to reach for my dagger, to rid him of the knowledge that gleamed in his too-pale eyes. I resisted, knowing that I needed his magic first and then I could decide if he needed to die for what he knew.

Fallon would look at me very differently if she knew I'd guided her mother to the decision to marry her off and not just been another victim in her schemes.

"Of course not, my King," Eryx said, dipping his head forward in a mockery of a bow. "Only commenting on the incredible luck you've been gifted with. A wife you find tolerable outside of a mating bond is practically unheard of. If only all of us could be graced with the same fortune."

"Good," I said, nodding even though I knew his statement had only been a play of words. It was also as good as I would get as a declaration that he wouldn't share the information he knew, because nothing was truly sacred in the Court of Shadows when Mab would torture her own allies for information. "Does that mean you will help me sneak her out of Tar Mesa?"

He worried his lip in thought. "I don't suppose you would be open to hearing about how displeased that will make your future wife? If she is anything like Rheaghan, she'll be furious that you forced her to abandon her loved one here," he said, stating the obvious that I'd already considered. But I'd long since come to adopt the mindset that it was far better to ask forgiveness than permission, especially when it involved a person's safety and well-being. In time, I had to trust that Fallon would come to know I had only done what was necessary to remove her from a dangerous situation while simultaneously solidifying our rule and doing what I could to keep my people safe from outside influences.

"I think you'd better give me a satchel of extra sleep dust for the journey, just in case," I said, earning a frustrated smile.

"For all that you claim Fallon is like her uncle, I think you fail to see how like him *you* are," he said, making his way to the door of his bedroom. He gripped the handle and tugged the door open with one hand as he pulled a satchel from his pocket that he kept at the ready, holding it out for me to take with me in spite of his disapproval. "One of these days, it will land you in trouble, just like it did him."

The warning sat heavy on my chest as I followed Eryx into the hall, knowing that he spoke of Rheaghan's stubborn unwillingness to accept the fact that his sister was a lost cause. That the cursed gem had changed her so fully and completely that there was no chance of the sister he knew ever returning.

It would make Fallon's forgiveness all the more beautiful when it came, knowing what we were able to overcome when we were together.

"I'll keep that in mind," I said as I pulled the key to my room from my pocket. The space behind my bedroom door was too quiet as I stepped up to it, pausing to listen for any activity. Fallon had seemed to settle, the sounds of her rage no longer heard from the hallway. I inserted the key and turned it, waiting for Fallon to react to the sound of my return. It seemed to echo through the halls, bouncing off the stone in the otherwise silent space. "Better let me go first," I said, motioning Eryx back.

He raised his hands, backing to the other side of the hall as if he greatly feared the woman that waited for me on the other side.

I couldn't even say I blamed him.

With a deep breath, I steeled myself for whatever attack may wait on the other side. Pushing the door open quickly in case she might be waiting just on the other side, I winced when the door bounced off the wall as it flung open fully without obstruction.

Fallon stood before the daybed, her chest heaving with exertion. Her fingers bled, the tips rubbed raw and scraped, and my gaze dropped to them immediately. The scent of her blood flooded my nostrils, stealing over my senses and bringing temptation to the surface. She may not have been my mate, her skin solely marked with the color of the Shadow Court, inky trails of darkness winding up her arms to indicate that her mate was likely a human, but that didn't stop my desire.

"Fallon . . ." I said, my voice trailing off. I was proud of the concern that laced the tone, at the worry over her injuries and what she might have done to herself in my absence, and how it superseded the violence simmering in my blood for her one-day mate, whom I would murder the moment she spoke of him.

She screamed, turning and grabbing the heavy vase from the bedside table. I barely had time to duck before she hauled off, twisting her entire body with the force of her throw. It soared over my head, crashing against the opposite wall in the hallway just beside Eryx's shoulder. The God turned to look in shock at the impression it had made on the stone, his face twisting into a scowl as I followed his stare. Confusion knitted my brow as I considered the strength required to damage the porous surface. The vase had been crystalline, meaning it should have merely shattered on impact.

Instead . . .

I swallowed, spinning as Eryx's eyes widened when he turned back to face me. I shifted to Fallon, the blur of her form launching at me in anger. I caught her up in my arms when she was airborne, ducking my head as she extended those bloodied fingertips from her clenched palms and aimed for my eyes. "Fallon!" I shouted, wrenching her hands off me as I twisted her in my grip. I spun her in midair, forcing her to face away from me as she struggled. It was like trying to contain a summer storm, her skin warm to the touch as if her anger heated her very blood.

It felt like trying to hold on to the sun itself.

"I will *not* be locked away like I'm your property!" she spat, weaponizing the words I'd given her in frustration. While I didn't mean them in the truest sense of the word, I also did not intend to share her or allow her choices to bring herself harm.

Did that not equate her to something I owned, jealously hoarding and protecting her for myself like treasure?

"Would you just listen to me?" I asked, keeping my voice gentle as I wrestled her to the bed. She thrashed against it, fighting me every step of the way. She rose up onto her hands and knees, attempting to crack my nose with the back of her head. I shifted to the side in time to avoid the worst of the blow, tucking her head into the crook of my neck and pinning her with a hand to the front of her throat. She snarled, twisting, her teeth bared. "You will belong to me, but I will be yours in turn, Sunfire. All I ask is that you give us the time we need to get there," I said, the snarl dropping off her face for a moment of confusion as she studied me. Taking advantage of her moment of stillness, I twisted her to the bed on her back, straddling her hips and pinning her arms above her head. "Eryx!"

The God came into the room at my summons, Fallon's eyes widening as she took in the other man. "I'm not interested in a three-way today. Try again later," she gritted out, bucking her hips as if she could dislodge me.

My own growl rose up in my throat, vibrating in my chest as Eryx grinned, looking back and forth between the two of us. "You will not touch him today. You will not touch him tomorrow. You will not touch him *ever*," I said, leaning toward Fallon's face and issuing the order. "I do not fucking share."

The little monster tipped her head to the side, smiling up at me as if she'd found my weak point and planned to use it to her every advantage. She shifted slightly, making me tense as I prepared for a fight. Instead, she raised a leg behind me, bending it at the knee and stroking her bare foot down Eryx's hip. The God's eyes protruded as he stifled a laugh, his deep chuckle unable to be contained as he touched the arch of her foot with a single teasing finger meant to drive me to rage.

He let his laugh loose when I reached behind me to slap his hand away, warning flashing in my eyes. "Oh, I *like* her," he said, earning a pleased smile from the woman I felt certain would be the end of me.

I wrapped my hand around the front of her throat, drawing her attention back to me forcefully. I nodded to the God, who stepped up beside her, staring down at Fallon in apology.

"Do it now," I ordered, anxious to be out of this court and away from temptation. The more men tempted Fallon, the more likely I would be to commit murder and be stuck paying penance in the Shadow Court.

"Sorry, love," Eryx said, reaching into his pocket and grasping an entire handful of sand. Fallon's eyes flashed wide, her mouth opening with a scream as the dust fell onto her face. She silenced immediately, blinking back the grit in her eyes as the dust settled, making itself at home in her body as the fight in her limbs went limp.

"Don't fight it," I said, leaning forward to touch my forehead to hers. I was all too aware of the way Eryx watched the interaction, measuring the tenderness as Fallon's sleepy eyes filled with fear. "Let me keep you safe," I said, releasing my hold on her throat and hands now that her body was lost to the tiredness that no one could resist. Her head tipped to the side as if she couldn't hold it up anymore, her eyes drifting closed slowly as I petted her raven hair gently.

I'd do whatever it took to keep my word to her, to protect her from even herself.

Getting her out of this place of horrors had to be my priority, not the friends she would leave behind.

"You breathe a word of what you learned today, to anyone, and you will find the water you drink poisoned. Make no mistake," I warned Eryx, shifting Fallon into position so that I could carry her out.

He smiled, nodding his assent. "Wouldn't *dream* of it," he said, a smirk playing at his mouth.

Fuck.

Twelve

ETAN

I carried Fallon's sleeping form out the front doors of Tar Mesa, ignoring the hushed whispers of the other courts as they watched us depart. I wished I could say it would bother me that they weren't being permitted to leave alongside us, that I knew exactly what they thought of me as I fled the scene with Mab's daughter in my arms.

As soon as news reached them of our impending nuptials, which would be completed the moment we arrived in Vallania, the capital of the Summer Court, they would think I'd been aware of Mab's plans to execute Rheaghan. They'd call me a Kingslayer, a man who betrayed all sense of honor in his pursuit of power. It wouldn't matter that it hadn't been my intention.

The horses were waiting for us as I stepped out the doors, along with the few members of my court who had come to the Tithe with us. Terence stood between two horses, holding the reins loosely clasped as he waited. His eyes widened as he took in the sight of me making my way toward him, clearly not expecting Fallon to be fast asleep. "Is she alright?" he asked, staring down at the woman who would soon be his queen. His opinions of her, as her mother's daughter, were irrelevant next to the duty that was his for the rest of his life now. To serve was the most important aspect of our lives, loyalty to those who controlled the court and kept us out of chaos, no matter what hatred stirred in his heart for the woman he didn't know. It was unfortunate that not all among the Summer Court would put duty before all else in the way Terence would, and I knew better than most that Fallon would have an uphill battle in earning the approval of my people.

Of *her* people, by blood—no matter how they wanted to ignore that fact.

"Just sleeping. I wanted to leave without a fight," I said, giving him a look that communicated just what Fallon would have thought of my plan to escape with her without allowing her to say her goodbyes.

He nodded, pursing his lips as he looped the reins over his arm, letting them settle into the crook of his forearm. The horses had been trained well enough that they wouldn't budge anyway, but the last thing we needed was a discomfited horse racing off when I tried to settle Fallon at the front of the bareback pad. We'd have to travel the beginning of our journey without a saddle in order for us to both be able to ride comfortably, and it was only through luck that I'd brought my gelding, who was far more likely to tolerate the extra weight because he was large enough to do so. Thunder was the color of night, his mane and tail a streak of white against the ebony color of his crest. The draft horse had been used to pull carts when he was younger, his size and stocky build making him the perfect horse for heavy lifting.

I might have brought my stallion under different circumstances, if it had not been for the knowledge that the horses would be largely cooped up in the stables during our stay. He'd never fared well when confined.

"I can hand her up to you," Terence said, holding out his hands as if I should give Fallon over to him. I eyed him warily, glancing at the horse beside me and knowing there was no way I could mount with her in my arms. Without a saddle, I didn't stand a chance without a leg up.

"Give me a leg up," I said to him, glancing toward one of the women in our company. "Marceline, could you hold her for a moment?" I asked, dreading the knowing smirk that crossed her features. Marceline was one of the few people I trusted fairly implicitly, a friend of mine and Rheaghan's from childhood. We'd all grown up together, though she hadn't been raised by Rheaghan's mother in the same way I had been; she'd come into our lives after Mab had been cursed and never got to know her before. Her father had served in the Summer Court forces, rising to a rank that meant he was in near-constant communication with the Primordial Queen herself, until she disappeared overnight.

I'd never hear the end of it.

She handed the reins for her own horse to one of the other women in our party, regardless of what she might have seen in my hesitance to allow Terence to touch Fallon. I hoisted Fallon into Marceline's arms, allowing the Fae woman to support my bride's weight as I hurriedly stepped into the cupped hands Terence held out as he knelt, bouncing my weight up three times. On the third, he lifted me higher and I swung my other leg over Thunder's rear, settling in at the back of the bareback pad and patting Thunder's neck gently.

Marceline adjusted Fallon in her grip, lifting her with strength that most Fae women did not possess by nature, but Marceline was more determined than many to be at home with the soldiers. She worked out and trained with us when she could simply thrive in politics because of her father's rank, with little regard for the fact that others would claim she should be weaker, that she shouldn't show up the men who thought they needed to prove themselves.

I reached down to grab Fallon under the arms, hauling her limp form up onto Thunder's back. The horse adjusted his position, shifting his weight from one leg to the other as I settled her in front of me. I tipped her back toward me, leaning her weight into my chest as Terence swung the reins over Thunder's head and I picked them up, bunching them into one hand so I could keep my other arm wrapped around Fallon's waist to prevent her from falling. Her head lolled to the side, her cheek pressed into my chest feeling like it fit there, nestled into the crook of my shoulder as if it had been carved specifically for her.

If I'd been a better man, I might have paused to allow that sliver of guilt I felt to permeate me, to change my course of action. I might have hesitated to take away her will and manipulate her unconscious body to get her safely out of Tar Mesa without causing a scene neither of us could afford.

As it stood, I was self-aware enough to know I only felt hints of certain feelings others possessed in multitudes. It wasn't so much that I lacked a conscience; I lacked the ability to prioritize where it guided me. I had spent so much of my time justifying my actions to myself, and all the harm I'd caused in my appearance of an alliance with Mab, that I'd lost the ability to feel true guilt over them. The ends justified the means, because it was the only way I could keep believing that what I was doing was right, and that role I'd played had been my entire life's purpose for so long that I *needed* it to be what was right.

My sense of right and wrong had all but disappeared in my centuries at Mab's service and without ever finding my mate. It felt as if she might have been my moral compass, distant and impossible to reach. It seemed unfathomable that in my centuries of life, she had yet to come into existence, because such a timeline without the appearance of one's mate was unheard of. To go so long was to welcome the madness that came from a soul being split for too long, but I'd never felt even a twinge of my mate's soul.

When others had felt their mates on the other side of the Veil, I'd felt nothing but emptiness. There was no completion to be found for me, and maybe that was why I didn't care that what I was doing with Fallon was objectively wrong.

Fate had deprived me of the mate I was promised. It seemed only fair I'd steal a wife for myself instead.

She wouldn't have a choice but to forgive it, given enough time with me. We all blustered and claimed we could hold a grudge, but only the worst offenses were worth centuries of anger. While we all held our grudges against Mab for obvious reasons, few other conflicts were capable of withstanding the test of time. A few months, a year or maybe a few, that was a blink of an eye compared to what we would have together.

I adjusted my seat, lightly squeezing my calves against Thunder's side and making a quiet clicking sound. Terence and Marceline mounted quickly, joining the band of seven others who needed to return to Vallania. We would go our separate ways soon enough, Fallon and I destined to make the journey to the capital once we reached the fringes of the Summer Court. We needed to put some distance between us and Tar Mesa if we wanted to escape before the Lunar Witch, Imelda, realized we were stealing away with her charge. As soon as we had enough distance between us, we would venture off on our own for the sole purpose of following Summer Court traditions.

The others would ride ahead to alert the Summer Court of Rheaghan's death and the upcoming wedding, giving them a head start in the preparations that would be needed. A wedding and a funeral rite so close together was wrong on so many levels, but there was no way around it under the circumstances. We would have barely a breath between mourning Rheaghan and all that he'd done to keep our people safe, and celebrating the marriage that would guide us into the future.

"You'll take her on the Bridal Walk?" Marceline asked, guiding her horse up beside mine. Thunder tolerated very few getting too close to him, but he had an adoring relationship with her much smaller mare, Lady, that almost made me feel bad he was gelded and couldn't act on that love.

"Yes," I said, nodding as I met her eyes.

The smirk from earlier returned to her face, and I turned my gaze straight forward to avoid the questions I knew were coming. "Never pictured you as the marrying kind, Etan," she said, choosing instead to poke at the situation and prod for weak spots.

"Neither did I, but Mab hardly asked for my opinion," I said, all too aware of the listening ears nearby. Marceline pressed her mouth into a line, suppressing a laugh and biting back the words that would likely call me out on my half-truth. It wasn't a *lie* by any means—Mab hadn't asked me for my opinion.

She hadn't needed to.

"I'm sure she didn't *ask*," Marceline whispered, steering Lady closer so that the words could remain between us. Our feet nearly touched, toes pointed to the sky to keep our seats as we guided our horses over the salt dunes. I glanced over my shoulder to make sure no one was close enough to hear, but she'd timed her question well and the others were distracted by lively conversation, the joy of being out of Mab's palace tangible. "But I'm sure you could have dissuaded her if you wanted. You have more control over her than anyone."

I did.

I did and that made me feel horrible for all the things I couldn't control. Like I should have been trying harder to protect everyone, and not only the people of my court. But to do so would compromise my position, would put her trust at risk when I needed it to keep us all safe.

The ends justified the means, even if that meant I was sacrificing the people of the other courts to her ways to save mine.

Fallon stirred lightly, nuzzling into my chest as if she took as much comfort in my embrace as I did hers. Marceline didn't miss the motion, her gaze narrowing in on Fallon's stunning face. "You're so fucked," she said, laughing as she pulled Lady away and guided her back to the others to avoid attracting unwanted attention from some of the members of our traveling party who were slightly less trustworthy with sensitive information.

When we'd passed the salt dunes, I opened a palm and slid my blade across it, offering my blood to the shadows to combat the light we would bring into the court. Light and dark were out of balance in this place, and the shadows craved that light more than even we did. It took something from us to do so, but I called to the light around us, drawing it off the moon and the reflection of it against the sand and salt surrounding us. The sunwalk opened up, a tunnel of blinding brilliance as I guided Thunder through the opening.

And it bathed us in absolute, pure white.

Thirteen

FALLON

There was something warm pressed against my spine, the heat of it like a searing brand seeping through the cold that had permeated my entire being. I snuggled deeper, sinking into that unfamiliar warmth until a deep sound of contentment reached me. My head felt fuzzy, pulsing with the beginning of a groggy headache at my temples. I groaned as I forced my eyes to open, blinking back from the blinding brightness in front of me.

The sun began to rise over the mountainside across the valley. The land before us dipped low, giving me a panoramic view that was covered in cliffs, in mountains and rolling hills that seemed to defy possibility. The valley was filled with fog, making the center of it all seem bathed in mist. The mountains were bare of trees, the earth a deep red with bright green moss and grass, as I dropped my hand to the ground beside me and buried my fingers in the squishy, sponge-like surface.

It was somehow softer than the grass I'd felt in Nothrek, in the crunchy, dying nature as it gave way to the coming winter. I squinted against the brightness of the sunrise, the way it painted the clouds overhead with a distinct display of yellow and gold, bathing everything in warmth. My face heated beneath it, and though I had to close my eyes to shut out the light that they weren't used to, I still basked in the warmth of it on my skin.

My hand brushed against something as I raised it from the ground, the rough fabric making me open my eyes and study what I'd touched. A leg clad in trousers rested beside me, wrapped around my hips and hooked around my body like a cocoon. I twisted, staring in shock at Etan's peaceful face. He'd propped himself up against a tree, the land behind me far more forested. The earth was covered in fallen leaves, the colors a myriad of reds, yellows, and oranges. It was so like Nothrek had been when I first emerged from the tunnels, but somehow so much *more*. His eyes were closed, his breathing deep and even with sleep, and he was completely lost to the waking world that was somehow so much more vivid than anything I'd ever dreamed of.

This was the world I was meant to explore.

I eased myself out from his grasp, carefully getting to my feet and putting some distance between us so that I could attempt to remember where I was and how the fuck I'd gotten here. The memory slammed into me so suddenly that I gasped, pressing my hand to my mouth to try to catch the sound before it could wake Etan. I scrambled to my feet, taking a few steps away from the man who had fucking kidnapped me while I slept. We were alone, no traces of anyone else nearby. With my back to the sun, I missed the moment it finally crested the horizon, too busy studying the land behind me.

Given the clear signs of a season in front of me, I knew that the area behind Etan had to be the Autumn Court. The Shadow Court was nestled within the Winter Court. I knew only from passing conversations I'd overheard and the stories Imelda had shared that the Winter Court and Autumn Court made up the Unseelie Court, that the Summer and Spring Courts were the Seelie Courts, putting them at direct odds throughout their history before the evil that was Mab had united them against a common enemy.

The back of my neck tingled, a buzz of magic against my skin where my hair had been pulled to the side and draped over one shoulder carefully. It was knotted there, tied with a ribbon that I had no recollection of owning or seeing in my rooms at Tar Mesa. I touched shaking fingers to the back of my neck, too fearful to turn and see what I might find behind me. There was nothing there to explain the touch, nothing present aside from the strange warmth of my skin. It came from both outside of me and within me, radiating around me like a cycle as I turned slowly to face the valley once more.

The sun of Alfheimr beat down on my skin for the first time, and I twisted my hand in the sunlight that seemed to shimmer with a warm, golden hue that wasn't like the aura of gold that surrounded Estrella when she touched her magic. This was simply a golden sparkle along my skin, like someone had bathed me in flecks of gold dust. My skin was fair beneath the pulsing, shimmering glow as I shoved my sleeves up farther, tipping my face up to the sun to enjoy the warmth for the first time when my entire body wasn't being torn to pieces and remade during the change from human to Fae.

I drew in a deep breath, my lungs filling with something ethereal as my insides warmed against the cold that had entrapped me for the entirety of my life. It chased away the darkness lingering within me, clinging to the corners of my mind and my very being and lighting my soul aflame.

I originally hadn't thought I would recognize it when it came, hadn't thought I would understand what it felt like at my fingertips, until I felt it dancing along my skin, a silent question posed in every touch.

Magic.

Magic that was so much stronger than the faint, tiny whispers I'd gotten trapped in the Shadow Court with Imelda's warding to keep it at a distance. I didn't dare reach out to answer, even without Mab watching over my shoulder, and instead turned to make sure Etan was still sleeping. He'd lolled to the side without my body to keep him pinned to the tree, his head dangling in a way that looked uncomfortable. He could wake at any moment, find me glowing in the sunlight.

I couldn't risk being seen as I discovered exactly what magic would answer, and I let my eyes drift closed slowly as I thought back to all the times Imelda had explained the concept of warding. She'd taught me how to lean in to the warding she'd placed on me at birth, the very same one she'd refreshed as I lay on the snow of Alfheimr, screaming in pain as I shifted from human to Fae, and after I'd been taken to Tar Mesa. I'd witnessed Estrella's powers make a slave of her, watched them bind her to a will that was not entirely her own. The consequences for her had been far-reaching, including the mate that she would lay down her life for.

I would never allow myself to be controlled in the same way, doing whatever it took to maintain autonomy over my own being. I wouldn't be beholden to a court because of some magic flowing through my veins when I'd spent my entire life existing as a person without it, wouldn't let my carefully maintained composure be altered in the name of some birthright.

The call of the magic was too strong to ignore, and I needed Imelda to strengthen her wards if I had any hopes of keeping it contained in the future. It existed within me, but it was a mirror for the magic of Faerie that surrounded me. All of our kind who possessed magic had it both within our blood and in the world around us, and Imelda referred to it as a symphony that required both aspects to achieve true beauty.

I reached out with my consciousness, touching the warding that Imelda had placed on me. I didn't know what it disguised, nor did I care to, but I stroked against the wall it formed between my magic and the magic of Alfheimr. It shriveled away within me as I wrapped it in a firm hand, grasping it and pulling it with all my might. I shoved it back inside the barrier of Imelda's warding, a thing that would need to be refreshed very soon, and locked it away until I wanted to use it.

Shoved it into the deepest recesses of my mind until I was truly alone and could risk getting to know what existed within me.

I opened my eyes to watch the sunlight on my skin wink out like tiny fires in the night, the golden hue fading from my fair skin and leaving me feeling suddenly cold. There was no doubt what had triggered the strengthening of the magic, and what had burned through Imelda's warding so quickly.

The sun.

I swallowed as I lowered myself to the ground, sitting with my legs dangling over the rounded edge of the mountaintop as I waited for Etan to wake. He might be my husband soon enough, but that didn't mean he got to lay claim to the parts of me I would keep for myself.

I just needed to find a way to bring Imelda to the Summer Court, and I needed to do it quickly.

Before everyone learned the truth that there was magic in my veins after all—that it burned inside me after a lifetime in darkness.

Fourteen

ETAN

I woke with a start, the realization that my arms were empty sending a pang of panic through me. I couldn't explain this intense knowledge that something was missing, that a part of me had walked away while I slept. We lingered at the edge of the Autumn Court, the Summer Court sprawled before me like a beacon welcoming me home.

The place where Fallon had once slept was empty now, the only companion nearby the presence of Thunder where I'd left his reins tied around a tree trunk in the shade behind me. He looked like he didn't want to keep moving, like the sweltering heat that waited for us in the Summer Court was something he dreaded, and I couldn't blame him entirely in spite of my desire to make it to my home.

We would need to pass through the desert before we could get to the lush center of the Summer Court with its flowing waters and ocean breeze, but this was a journey Fallon and I needed to take before our coronations.

"Fallon?" I asked, getting to my feet and spinning in disbelief. I couldn't believe the woman would be foolish enough to wander off in the middle of the Unseelie Court, that she would show so little regard for her own safety that she would wander alone in an unfamiliar, dangerous place without any magic or weapons to protect her. We'd separated from the others before making camp for the night, as soon as we'd crossed the boundary out of the Winter Court. They'd taken the direct route to Vallania, leaving Fallon and me to take the long way alone.

My hand dropped to the scabbard on my hip, searching for my sword. It was still there, the familiar weight of it pressed into me, but my gaze dropped to the strap at my ankle and the distinct absence of the dagger I kept there.

"Fucking Gods," I cursed, storming to the edge of the mountain. I looked over the ledge, searching the steep path for any sign of Fallon's footprints. The dust had not moved, and I reached up a tentative hand to weigh the boundary between courts, to test it in the way that I'd seen Rheaghan do so many times. My eyes drifted closed as I let the magic of it sink into me, a vibration running down the boundary like a spider's net, searching for prey in the form of my errant betrothed, who couldn't seem to stay where I put her.

Something recoiled not far down the line, and I turned to my right to peer through the Autumn Court trees there. My feet followed, guiding me to where Fallon waited in the shade as if she wanted to avoid the sun on her skin, and with how pale she was, that might have been a wise choice.

She stood at the edge, running her fingers over the boundary and staring at her hands in surprise.

She could feel it.

The boundary that existed between the Unseelie and Seelie Courts was an invisible wall from a bygone era. Only those with a predisposition to either throne could feel it, could know when someone passed through. It served as an alarm to protect against those who did not belong, protecting us when we'd fought in wars that seemed so foolish now as we looked back in hindsight.

I ran my hand over the boundary as I approached, letting the vibrations of my touch ripple down the surface. She turned to me as she felt it, and a smug smile stole over my face.

If I'd had any doubts as to whether I'd made the right choice, the boundary washed them away with a single moment.

It recognized her.

She looked different in the light, brighter somehow, as if she was always meant to be outside the darkness. She was beautiful in the dark, but the light did something to her that made her somehow *more*. All the Summer Court Fae were similar, a sense of peace existing within them that came with proximity to the source of our magic, however minimal it may be in the Sidhe, who only held a tendril.

"Are we the only ones who left Tar Mesa?" she asked instead of greeting me. Her face was pinched, her features hard as she looked at me in a way that communicated her anger over what I'd done. She didn't need to yell to tell me that, her emotive face offering everything her words did not.

"The rest of the Summer Court left along with us," I said, holding my position. I wouldn't force my proximity on her when it wasn't necessary, knowing that this simmering attraction between us would pull us together in time, no matter how much she may try to fight it.

"Then where are they?" she asked, crossing her arms over her chest. She strode back toward the place where I'd slept and the horse waiting there, breezing past me without stopping to make sure I followed.

"They went ahead, took the easy paths. They'll reach Vallania within two days," I explained, following after her. I trailed a short distance behind her, close enough to reach out and touch her if I lunged, but not so close as to breathe down her neck and make her uncomfortable. "It is customary that we make this journey alone to prove our worth."

She sighed, spinning to face me with a sudden burst of speed. She stumbled a little, the movement far less than coordinated. I narrowed my eyes on her face but didn't move to help her, allowing her to right herself and shrug off the clumsy movement.

I had to imagine that becoming Fae after a lifetime as a human came along with some adjustments, that the changes in her body would take getting used to, but I'd never seen her move with anything other than carefully crafted grace before.

Other than the moment where she'd shattered the vase, anyway.

"Why are we not taking the easy paths?" she asked, making her way to Thunder. The horse extended his neck, reaching for her and nudging her with his muzzle. She patted his neck gently, smoothing the hair there with tenderness instead of fear despite his size. "And why the fuck is there only one horse?"

"Can't have you riding off now, can I?" I asked, quirking a brow at her. She'd carefully danced around what I'd done, avoiding the reality of me smuggling her out of Tar Mesa while she slept.

"What exactly would be the point in running away?" she asked, shaking her head as if the suggestion was foolish. "If my options are you or Mab, I think I know which one is less terrifying."

"Ouch," I said, rubbing my chest as if she'd wounded me. She only rolled her eyes in response, fidgeting with Thunder's mane as she worked it into a running braid. The gelding looked at her from the corner of his eye, turning his head to push at her side in response. It hadn't been her desire to stay in Tar Mesa that drove me to believe she'd return.

It was the witch we'd left behind, the one I knew without a doubt I needed to separate her from if I wanted to have any chance of getting to know the Fallon that I knew was in there. She was dependent on Imelda, on the relationship they'd formed over their years in Nothrek, and I suspected there was a greater dependence to that relationship than I could even begin to understand.

In order for Fallon to come into her own, she needed to leave her past where it belonged—at least for a little while.

She swatted Thunder away playfully without a care, turning him to face forward once more. "If that is the worst I say to you by the end of this, then count yourself lucky. There may come a day where I aim to make you cry."

The distinct lack of venom in her words was nearly shocking, the statement coming as a simple fact. "I'll keep that in mind. I can hardly expect you not to burn me in our eternity together, Sunfire," I said, crossing my arms over my chest as I leaned back into the tree opposite where Thunder was tied and watched her work.

"Don't call me that," she spat, the nickname bringing out the worst of the ire that she'd kept carefully buried. It had struck a chord within her, something she hated brought to the surface. But instead of wanting to appease her anger by never using it again, it felt like the kind of wound I needed to poke at. Like it was responsible for so much of Fallon's odd behavior when she shut away her cares.

"Does it frighten you?" I asked, crossing my ankles as I studied her. She paused, her hands stilling on Thunder's mane, though she didn't deign to look at me. "To know how hot your temper flares? To know what you would do for the ones you love? To know how you could light up the world if you let yourself?"

She turned to look at me slowly, her hazel eyes burning with rage and nostrils flared. "I would not light up the world," she said, her voice laced with warning. "I would burn it to the ground if given a chance and leave nothing but ashes in my wake. I know myself well enough to know that whatever I am, it is something to be contained. I don't trust myself to remain in control if I unleash my rage on this world."

"You cannot cage a wildfire," I said, pushing off the tree trunk to approach her.

She turned to face me fully, spreading her feet to shoulder-width apart as if we would fight. Given what had happened in her bedroom before Eryx forced her to sleep, I couldn't exactly fault her for the assumption. There were probably a great many altercations in our future as husband and wife, and I looked forward to ending them with our slickened bodies fighting in the most carnal way.

"Then maybe you should put it out," she said, the words striking me in the chest. They were laced with self-hatred, with self-doubt and uncertainty. I wanted nothing more than to reach out and soothe whatever old hurt lingered there, and I watched as her fingers rose to the scar at her eyebrow, as if on instinct.

"How did you get that?" I asked, making her drop her hand suddenly.

"That's none of your fucking business," she spat, but she squinted her eyes against the light. "It gives me headaches to this day. Imelda makes me a poultice to soothe the ache. Did she go ahead with the others? Why are we not traveling together?" she asked again.

"We are not traveling together because you and I must make the customary journey of Kings through the mountains, so that we may be crowned when we arrive in Vallania. It is how we earn the right to rule from the magic of our court itself," I said, untying Thunder's reins from the tree. I led him to a fallen log and dropped them to the ground, knowing he would not move as I stepped onto the log and hoisted myself onto his back.

I reached down, holding out a hand for Fallon so that I could lift her up. Riding Thunder was far less than ideal—he was too tall, and Fallon would need to give me a leg up or we'd have to find something to stand on in order to mount again, but the alternative was a horse who would tire too easily carrying our combined weight.

"And Imelda will be waiting for me there?" she asked again, eyeing my hand. It became clear that she would not mount until I answered.

"Imelda is still in Tar Mesa," I said, watching as her eyes widened. She stumbled back a single step, as if the words were a physical blow.

"I need her."

"Why?" I asked, forcing her to close her eyes in frustration.

"I just . . . need her."

I reached forward, grasping Fallon's forearm and using it to hoist her up in front of me, even though it was a very uncomfortable way to get her mounted. "I think it is high time you learned to stand on your own without your witch to guide you. There are witches in Vallania who can make the poultice for your headaches," I snapped, wrapping my arms around her and urging Thunder into a steady walk forward. Fallon fell silent, her body shaking with anger.

I'd known it would be the case, but it didn't matter to me.

Fifteen

FALLON

One fucking horse.

I sighed, squirming and trying to put some distance between Etan and me. He kept one arm slung around my hip casually, using it to pull me back. I couldn't even be too angry about it; my forward position probably put me too far from Thunder's center of gravity and made it uncomfortable for him. I reached down and patted the horse's withers, settling into the discomfort of Etan's chest pressed into me. Riding bareback meant there was absolutely no barrier between us, my ass nestled into his groin so that there was very little left to the imagination as to how we might fit together if I were to ever agree to make this more than simply a political arrangement.

Given his perspective of what was required to be an equal to him, I very much doubted that would happen. He might think it acceptable to claim ownership over me, but I was not one to allow that to settle.

I was no man's property, no man's possession, and anyone who thought to change that simply because he felt entitled would wake up with a knife between his eyes.

"Tell me about your home," Etan said, his voice far too casual for the awkward silence that had descended over us since we started the journey through the Summer Court. The sandy terrain was difficult for Thunder to navigate, his steps slow and cautious as we descended the path down toward the valley. The earth was dry and red, the cliffs beside us pointed and jagged. Faces and animals and plants had been carved into the terracotta stone, a history of travelers who had come before us to mark our journey.

"I don't have a home," I said evasively, shrugging my shoulders with the truth of the words. I might have *had* a home and a family before, a place to rest my head and human parents who loved me, but I knew I could never go back there. I would never be welcomed back to the rebellion who hated the Fae, to the parents who would hardly recognize what had become of me. Even if Nothrek hadn't been filled with Mist Guard and other myriad soldiers who would have killed me on sight, I could never stand to see the disappointment in the faces of the people I loved. "Not anymore, anyway."

I couldn't stand the rejection I would find there, knowing that the very thing I had been born to, the thing I'd had no choice in becoming, would horrify them.

Etan sighed, his touch tightening on my waist in sympathy. "Your home is with me now, Fallon," he said, trailing off to let that sink in. "But I meant the home where you were raised. I'd like to know everything I can so I might prepare you for what is to come. I don't want anything to be too much of a shock, but I cannot help arm you with information without knowing much of anything about your past. Those I spoke to about you in Tar Mesa were either unwilling to share what they knew or didn't know much of anything. Even your handmaiden didn't seem to have much to say."

"Is this your desperate attempt to get me to open up to you?" I asked, wishing more than anything that this conversation had occurred in a place where I had an escape. I didn't want to sit with him and be forced to face the awkwardness of this, without a place to retreat if I bared too much of my soul and felt naked and vulnerable.

Etan chuckled, the warmth of the sound sinking inside me. I felt the rumble against my spine, the genuine humor in it, as if he found my snark entertaining. Not in a degrading way, like it was futile or useless, but like he genuinely enjoyed the path of our conversations and the unpredictability of what I spoke at any given moment. "I have been desperate for very little in my long life, Sunfire." He spoke the words above my head, the warmth of his breath surrounding me. It should have been impossible to feel it with the searing heat pressing down on us, especially given the sun as it beat down on my skin.

I feared I would be burned to a crisp by the time we reached Vallania, but after several hours in the sun since it had risen, I couldn't help but find peace in the slight golden hue, in the tan that was the first I'd ever had.

"But let me guess, you're desperate for *me*, right?" I asked, rolling my eyes toward the sun that I squinted at. It had cast a golden hue over the blue of the sky closest to it, a wash of pure, unfiltered light radiating in a halo around it. It was so similar to the sunkiss on my skin that I couldn't help but draw comparisons, remembering the feeling of magic on my skin before I'd shoved it into that wall Imelda had created.

"Would that make you feel better about sharing with me? If I said I was desperate to know everything about you and where you'd come from? Or is it just your body you expect me to be desperate for?" Etan asked, lifting his hand from my hip to snag my chin. He twisted my neck slowly, forcing me to give him my profile so that I could stare at him from the side of my eye as he leaned in and drew his nose up over the side of my jaw to press his lips to my temple sweetly. "Desperation makes fools of men, and I have no intention of ever being a fool for a woman who will not so much as speak to me."

I jerked away, my anger rising at the manipulation and games he seemed so inclined to play. His words were so at odds with the physical intimacy he showed, leaving me reeling with no hope of ever understanding exactly what he intended for me—what he wanted from this marriage. The mixed signals were the epitome of frustrating, and I wished I was capable of making the rest of our journey on foot to avoid his touch. "I'm glad we've established that," I hissed.

"You misunderstand me, Sunfire. I have no intention of being a fool for a woman who keeps me at a distance, but I would be desperate for the woman who was just as desperate for me," he said, and I couldn't help the way my head snapped back to stare at him with a furrowed brow.

"And you expect me to believe that's me? That I'm the one who brings you to your knees with all your claims of ownership," I argued, but the steel had left my voice. My breath felt uneven, altered by the intensity of his stare on my profile.

"You hear what you want to hear, Fallon," he said, shrugging as if disappointed in me. "Instead of focusing on the fact that I said I believe you're capable of earning my respect as an equal worthy of ruling an entire kingdom at my side, you've chosen to focus on my not knowing you well enough to trust you with that responsibility right this very moment. We barely know one another, Fallon. I am merely trying to bridge that gap for both our sakes."

I withered, shrinking in on myself and hating the logical explanation. "Your words were intended to hurt. You said them as cruelly as you could manage," I said, shoving away his attempt to reason with me about something that had been deeply personal.

"You're right. They were spoken in an attempt to get you to listen and understand the reality that we were going to leave Tar Mesa whether you liked it or not. No matter what you may think of it, Mab expects me to be responsible for both your safety and your behavior now, so I will not allow your actions to put everything I have worked to protect at risk. I have given centuries to doing everything I can to keep my people safe from the worst of Mab's impulses and lost a part of myself to do it. If you would stop to see me as anything more than your enemy, you would understand that you are now in that list of things I will work to protect," he said, dropping his arm back to my hip as I tensed.

"Bold words coming from one of Mab's allies," I spat, relishing the way his entire body turned solid behind me. My words had left their intended mark, striking as deep as he'd meant to hurt me.

Instead of spitting venom back at me, he only sighed and released all the tension into the dry air around us. "I think you might understand my position in Mab's life better if you got to know me and how I came to know both her and Rheaghan," he said, his hands tightening where they held me as if on reflex.

"What difference could that possibly make? Are the whispers I heard at Tar Mesa untrue? Was Mab not the one to name you Rheaghan's second-in-command? Did you not spy on your own King at her behest?" I asked. I didn't dare to admit to the hope surging within me, the tiny inkling that maybe everything wasn't what it seemed. Given all that I'd seen in my short time in Alfheimr, it seemed unwise to hope for decency in a world where the cruel prevailed.

"I can't remember my own parents," he said instead, the vulnerable words stated in such a matter-of-fact way that I froze in place. "Most of the Gods didn't generally have much interest in parenting, given the poor example they'd had from the Primordials. They dropped me off with Diell in the Summer Court when I was five years old. She wasn't with Khaos anymore—he disappeared long before the other Primordials and before Mab could be born, but since she had fallen in love with the Goddess Aesira, the two of them were raising Rheaghan and Mab together. Rheaghan and I were the same age, in spite of the fact that he was a God and I was the child of two Gods. Mab was less than two when I came to live with them, and I can still remember the way her brother doted on her."

"Look where that got him," I said, shaking my head from side to side to reject the tenderness of his admission.

"Rheaghan and Mab were just as much my siblings as they were each other's. I grew up alongside them, and Rheaghan and I eventually grew very close. When Mab adorned her crown with that gem, everything inside of her changed overnight. She was suddenly dismissive of Rheaghan's protectiveness, competitive with him in ways she hadn't been. She was the opposite of what Diell and Aesira were raising us all to be, but I was the only one who could penetrate that hatred. Rheaghan always theorized it was because I was her sibling by choice, because I had actively chosen to love her as my own sister, versus the rest of her family, who had just gotten stuck with her," he explained, and I furrowed my brow as I tried to understand how he'd come to choose Mab over Rheaghan. How his loyalty had strayed to the crueler of the two he considered siblings.

"And you continued to choose her? Even after all she's done?" I asked, swallowing with my fear that I'd been right. Hoping he was a decent male had been foolish, but I had such difficulty reconciling the gentler side of him with the cruel one—his soft center with the hard edges he liked to show like a preening peacock.

He continued on as if I hadn't spoken, not directly offering me an answer. "I think when the gem gifted her with those dark powers that twisted her up from the Princess of the Summer Court into what she is now, they also enhanced every insecurity she'd ever had. Took every notion that she didn't belong and blew them to new proportions. Mab is the most insecure woman I have ever had the displeasure of meeting, and that's why she needs constant reminders of her power. It's why she binds everyone to her will, so they cannot betray her when they realize she isn't infallible. Everyone but me," he said, and I raised a brow as I touched his hand with mine. The movement seemed to shock him, a moment of something tender lingering between us that hardened to sharpened edges as I processed his words.

"You and I are the only two people connected to Mab who are

not condemned to carrying one of her snakes within us. We are the only ones who are capable of directing her to produce change. It is a great gift of power she has given us, and I do everything I can to use it wisely while remaining free."

"You have free will, when so many others are not fortunate enough to be able to do as they please, and you spend that free will in her service anyway?" I asked, trying to wrap my mind around the fact that I was to spend the rest of my life standing next to someone who supported the Queen of Air and Darkness *willingly*.

"It is because I spend my life in so-called service to her that I am able to have free will even after all this time. There is something to be said for keeping your enemies close, Sunfire. Some wars are fought over centuries of deception before they ever reach the battlefield," he said, and I went quiet as I let those words sink into me. The implication in them was that he was actively standing against Mab, that he was working to undermine her.

But how could he pretend to support the woman who had killed his brother?

"So, you're not loyal to Mab?" I asked, unable to take an implication of anything as significant. The man was going to be my husband, and I needed to know where I stood. If I could trust him not to run to Mab with every development, or if he was as much my enemy as she was.

"No, Sunfire. I am loyal to the people of the Summer Court and to those I consider family. Mab stopped being my family centuries ago when I lost hope that she could be saved. After all she's done, I'm not even certain I want her to be. The little girl I remember would have rather died than seen what she became and what she's done. She was a good person, and I loved her." He paused, letting that revelation sink in for a moment. "But she's been dead for a long time."

Sixteen

ETAN

We rode in silence for a while, Fallon's body carefully controlled. I wouldn't have called it tense exactly, merely like she was somehow missing from her body. Like her mind had gone elsewhere, considering all that I'd told her and what that meant for her life in the Summer Court. She was infuriating, uncompromising when it came to attempting to understand the position I was in.

Choosing a Queen was no careless task, and when I'd thought to manipulate Fallon into being my wife, I hadn't intended to ever become King. I had greater concerns now, far more people relying on me than I'd had even days before. We were constantly at odds with the Unseelie Court, long before Mab had become the ruler of us all. Those old wounds didn't merely disappear when we were all held captive, and the fall of the Veil had only worsened those tensions.

Though my time at home had been limited between the fall and the time that Mab summoned us for the Tithe, we'd been forced to interact with the Unseelie Fae of the Winter and Autumn Courts more in those recent weeks than we had in centuries before. Fae fled their home courts in droves in an attempt to make it to the boundary between Alfheimr and Nothrek and board one of the ships to seek out their mates in the human realm.

But that meant that enemies who had not seen one another in centuries suddenly found themselves face-to-face, old tensions rising. While those of us who had Mab's attention weren't in any danger, because none would risk her wrath by killing us, the Sidhe who she would not miss were not so lucky. Fae had been killed over slights that had otherwise been forgotten, and it was all Rheaghan and I could do to try to keep our people safely tucked within the Summer Court— sending regiments to seek out Summer Court mates in Nothrek who were trained to survive and do no harm.

Fallon tipped her head to the sun for the hundredth time since we'd departed that morning, making our way down the rugged, sandy terrain in the scorching sun. She seemed to come alive beneath the light of it, appreciating it in a way that I hadn't seen before. "Did you miss the sun while you were locked away in the darkness of Tar Mesa?" I asked, referring to the way the shadows clung to every corner of the palace. While there was limited light outside during the day, Mab prohibited people from leaving the palace to enjoy it, knowing that her power lingered in the shadows and she did everything possible to maintain the integrity of her magic.

"You can't really miss what you've never had," she said, the strange words making my hold on her tighten.

"What do you mean? You've never seen the sun?" I asked, and the very notion of such a thing was so strange that I couldn't wrap my head around it. When I'd told Mab that I'd thought she needed to be exposed to the elements of her home court in order for her magic to surface, I hadn't realized that she may never have seen it.

"There were a few days when we were traveling through Nothrek to get to Alfheimr where I felt the sun on my skin," she admitted, her voice trailing low as if she realized how sad that made her life sound. "That was one of the first times I had seen the sun, though, the very first time I spent more than an hour in it. It wasn't a part of my daily life before, so it makes it hard to miss it daily even now."

"How is that possible?" I asked, thinking of what life must have been for the humans. Had they been plunged into darkness in truth? Had the erection of the Veil somehow influenced the sun in their realm? It felt like the human mates who *had* successfully returned to the Summer Court and not been caught up in Mab's schemes would have mentioned that, or their mates would have known once the bond was completed.

"I grew up in a human rebellion that had formed in opposition to the human monarchy and the influence of its new religion on us all. We long since stopped worshiping the Old Gods, but instead of just accepting that maybe we didn't *need* Gods at all, the King's great-great-grandfather, or whatever the fuck he was, placed the New Gods on a pedestal. Their will became all that mattered, and our lives were supposed to be spent in direct worship of them, to the point that there were strict expectations for us and how we spent our time. Particularly in the case of women. Most of us were sold to the highest bidder for marriage and breeding. The rebellion opposed that way of life," she explained with a heavy sigh.

"Why did that mean you couldn't see the sun?" I asked, unable to understand how her refusal to worship these New Gods had resulted in her life in the dark.

"We would have all been killed if we were discovered. We didn't follow the rules that the High Priests and Priestesses set out for us, and in doing so, that meant we would be executed. Estrella was condemned to death for refusing to marry the noble who chose her, and we would have all met that same fate on the surface. So we hid away in a network of tunnels in the caves of the mountains and formed a community there. It became a refuge for so many, and it was necessary. It allowed us to live as we saw fit, but there were sacrifices, too," she said, turning to look back at me. She licked her lips, and my gaze dropped to the drying skin there.

"Like seeing the sun," I said, watching as she nodded. I took my canteen from the saddlebag strapped across the back, guiding it to Fallon's mouth so that she could drink. For a moment, I thought her pride would make her refuse. That she would insist on holding it herself and the independence such a rebellion had instilled in her would be a block for us in the future. Instead, she let me guide her head back so the water could pour into her mouth, taking deep gulps that hinted at her strong thirst.

She'd known I had the canteens with me, had watched me drink countless times, but that independent streak had prevented her from asking for water.

Stubborn fucking woman.

I would need to check in with her regularly, clearly. To ask and offer to meet her needs so that she was not forced to *ask*. I noted it in my mind as something that I'd likely do for the rest of our lives. Having someone to care for and tend to was new territory for me, and I'd have to learn as I went.

"Like seeing the sun," she agreed, wiping her mouth with the back of her hand when she finally finished drinking. "For me at least. Most of the others alternated going to the surface to tend to the gardens that we'd hidden away on a mountaintop or going out to set traps or go hunting. But I had to stay within the wards Imelda placed on the tunnels to keep Mab from sensing me. We couldn't risk it even when the Veil was between us. We weren't sure how much she could sense with it in place."

She stroked her hands through Thunder's mane absently, gently tugging out any tangles she found in a way that he didn't seem to mind. She shifted as if her ass had started to hurt, and it occurred to me that it may have been her first time on horseback.

If she'd never left the tunnels, had she ever even been near a horse before? Had she ever been near any animals, aside from the dead ones hunters would have brought back?

A little bit of understanding bled into my knowledge of her stubbornness. "So you never left those tunnels," I said, my voice gentling as I shifted the reins into one hand and rested my other palm on her thigh—hoping she could feel it for the comfort I intended it to be and didn't read into it as something I didn't intend. She'd shared a bit about what life was like for women on the surface, but said little about what her rights as a woman might have been within the rebellion.

My jaw clenched at the thought of her being forced into a relationship with someone else—let alone someone she did not want for herself.

"What did you do with your time all these years?" I asked, wanting to get to know her. I knew she was selfless, staying hidden to avoid bringing Mab's forces down on her entire community. I knew she was loyal to her friends above all else. But I knew very little about what she wanted for *herself* and a part of me wondered if she'd ever even been given the opportunity to think about that.

"Imelda trained me as her apprentice in each of my lifetimes," she said, a wistful smile gracing her face. "I had human parents who lived there with us, and they did love me. But there was always a little bit of distance between us because they knew that I was different than the rest of them. Imelda made sure I always felt like I belonged . . ." She trailed off, and I barely refrained from flinching.

"Because you belonged with her," I said, suddenly understanding the attachment between the two women. Imelda may not have been her mother, but she'd been her guardian in every way that mattered.

She'd been her home.

Fuck.

Fallon nodded. "She taught me all about the different plants that the others brought back from the gardens and showed me how to preserve them for healing purposes. We stored them in what she called the apothecary, but it was really just this random alcove at the end of one of the tunnels that only a few of us knew about. She trained another girl too, because she knew there would come a time when she and I left the tunnels and someone needed to know how to use the herbs to heal without her."

"She trained you as a healer," I said, admiration lacing my tone. Few knew much about my upbringing prior to when I'd come to live with Rheaghan and Mab, but it sounded as if Fallon's knowledge was the human equivalent of what my mother had been gifted with as a Goddess. Levana was the Goddess of Witchcraft and Magic, and the legend stated that the witches had been one of her creations—that they worshiped her within their covens even still. She was far more their mother than she had ever been mine.

I possessed little of her magic within me, only successfully channeling it when I combined my father's magic with hers. They'd both been Gods, and unlike Caldris, I hadn't been blessed with enough magic to call myself a second-generation God.

"There must have been a lot of sick and injured in order for that to fill your days," I observed, feeling uncomfortable with the similarities that seemed to hit too close to home. We both had the same heritage in a way, Fallon through experience and me through blood, but neither of us alone had the magic it took to truly harvest such skills.

Living on the fringes of something great, without ever really being able to grasp it.

"It didn't take all my time," Fallon said, a wistful sort of smile transforming her face as her cheeks flushed with pink. She studiously kept her gaze forward, avoiding the stare that I kept on the back of her head—waiting for her to look at me. "I spent a lot of time writing in notebooks that Imelda would bring me after a team returned from a supply run. Dreaming of far-off lands and places that I would never get to see. The people of the rebellion were close, because we were so confined together. There was always entertainment that came in companionship, and that was highly encouraged in our community—the more partners the better, because there were fewer women than men. That was just for fun, though. I wasn't one of the women who did that as a day job, so to speak."

"Stop talking," I snapped, realizing that she was rambling. I knew it was probably her discomfort, but I couldn't decide what had provoked her to tell me about her history. I couldn't even decide if she was serious or if it was a cruel prank to push me away.

I had no business feeling possessive because of her past partners. It wasn't as if I'd been celibate, for fuck's sake.

"Are you a virgin, then?" she asked, turning to look at me with a smirk that made it clear that flush hadn't been out of embarrassment at all. She was *trying* to get under my skin, the little helfire. "Or are there plenty of previous partners that I'll have the pleasure of bumping into once we reach the Summer Court?"

"Ah, well, I—" I cut off, clearing my throat. "I hadn't thought that far ahead, but none of my previous partners were serious. They won't be an issue for you."

"Good. I'm not the jealous type. In fact, I think you'll find I'm quite open to sharing, but I do have a problem when others get possessive over something that doesn't belong to them either—"

"There will be no sharing, Sunfire. You're the only woman I need, and I would like for that to be reciprocated," I said, taking a deep breath so that I didn't show my entire ass and declare ownership of Fallon. While she hadn't outright told me her dreams, I was getting to know them slowly through the things she didn't say and the hints of what else was there.

"That sounded like it hurt," she said, snorting out a laugh that shook her entire chest.

"Do I get credit for trying?" I asked, grinning at her as I leaned forward and touched my forehead to hers. Her hazel eyes flashed with warmth, the cool tones seeming to burn as she sucked back a breath but didn't turn away. Her mouth was so close to mine that I could almost taste her, and I waited to see if she would close the gap between us.

She let her eyes drift closed instead, her words tumbling out as if she couldn't control them. She needed something to sever the moment, to pull her back from the desire that pulsed between us like something I could reach out and grasp in my hand. "I want to see the world," she said, making everything in me tense. "I don't want anything to tie me to one place. When I dreamed of far-off lands, it was with the hope that one day I would be able to start walking and never stop. Imelda gave me the skills I needed to survive that if I ever did it. You want monogamy, and I can't give that to you unless I *stay*. I don't want to be a prisoner anymore, Etan. I want to roam beneath the stars and know what it's like to be free and go where I want, when I want—"

I silenced her, leaning forward to touch my mouth to hers. The vulnerable words should have cautioned me away, a conflict rising between what the two of us needed. After our visit to the baths in a few days time, Fallon and I would be crowned King and Queen of the Summer Court. She would need to be present at my side in order for us to rule, and all she wanted was to leave.

But the admission was the first piece of vulnerability Fallon had offered me; it felt like a truce between us, and I had to have faith that we would be able to compromise. That we could see the world *together* and return home to the court that needed us when our business was finished.

She froze beneath my lips, her words dying off as I traced the seam of her mouth with my tongue. The angle of her head was awkward, but she turned her head more to face me fully as she let out a little sigh that I swallowed greedily. When the tension bled from her body on that sigh, I pressed closer and kissed her slowly, giving her the time necessary to change her mind. She didn't, instead releasing a little growl of frustration as she carefully swung her leg over the top of Thunder's neck and turned to the side. She repeated that process as he tensed beneath her, but she was as careful as she could be and mindful of his spine as she pulled her leg over. The movement had forced our mouths to separate, and I watched her to see what reaction I would get.

She reached up with a steady hand, touching the stubble on my jaw. Her skin was so soft it felt like silk, her hands uncalloused from hard labor the way mine were. She inched closer, tipping her head up and waiting for me to close the distance between us.

I smiled as I touched my mouth to hers again, wasting no time on preamble as I opened for her. She matched me, sliding her ass closer until she sat with her legs draped over mine and her core pressed to mine.

I groaned, but forced myself to pull away long enough to give her the reassurance she needed. "You're going to be my wife, not my prisoner, Sunfire," I said, the words a soft sigh. I wanted nothing more than to pull her down from Thunder's back and show her all that monogamy with me had to offer, but she'd given me something that mattered to her.

Something I had a feeling she didn't share with many.

"In my experience, there's little difference between the two," she said, her eyes uncertain as she studied me.

"A real marriage should be about compromising and seeing to one another's needs. I *have* to look after my people in the Summer Court and give them stability, but part of that requires me to go to all the different corners of Alfheimr and maintain relations with the nobles there. If your desires are to travel, then there's no reason we cannot do that. You'll have to be willing to compromise with me and understand that we may not be able to run off *all* the time, but I have no desire to lock you in a cage, Fallon. If we're able and things are stable, we can go wherever you want."

"You'd go with me?" she asked, and her shock was palpable.

"Sunfire, you couldn't keep me away," I said, smiling down at her as I tucked a stray lock of hair behind her ear on the side opposite of her braids.

"But you didn't ask for this or for me. Mab just dumped me on you, too—"

"Some of the best gifts are the ones you never asked for," I said, evading the truth and leaning into her more fully. I let her feel the press of me behind her, knowing that we were less than a day's ride from the first stop on our journey.

"You want me to look at you as a gift?" she asked, quirking her brow at me as if I was arrogant to think so.

I grinned, pulling her tighter into me so that she could feel me. She stilled in my arms, allowing the continued touch when she might not have only a few hours before.

"There are those who would view me as a great gift indeed," I said, grinning at the snort that she released.

"They must not have known you very well," she said, and had she not been stuck on a horse with me, I could almost picture her striding away.

Leaving me burning in her wake to prove her wrong.

Seventeen

FALLON

The journey through the Summer Court was long and arduous, the minutes passing into hours as we made our way over the desert plains. The heat was unbearable, sweat dripping down my temples and the back of my neck as we rode. Etan's warmth behind me didn't help matters—the man gave off as much heat as the hot springs in the tunnels of the rebellion. He seemed unfazed by it, even though sweat made his skin sheen when I turned to glance back at him.

He was acclimated to it, at home in it even, I imagined. Whereas I had grown up in the temperate climate of Nothrek, where we had four seasons and the summers never quite reached this level of heat, he'd spent centuries thriving in the humid air. I'd been belowground, insulated from the worst of the weather entirely, without any of the extremes that might have been more common on the surface. Even still, my hunch told me the hottest of weather in Nothrek was nothing next to this desert that never seemed to end in spite of the scent of ocean brine and the humidity to the air.

"This heat will take some getting used to," I grumbled as he led us up a particularly large sand dune. It was closer to the size of the mountain range I'd called home than what I'd imagined of the desert hills I'd only read about in the books Imelda shared with me.

He chuckled, the sound hoarse and appealing where it made his chest shake against my spine. He touched my head with his nose, his deep inhale of my scent something that should have felt wrong and too primal to be our reality, but somehow felt right in this form.

The differences between the humans and the Fae were somehow both minuscule and overwhelming all at once.

"Don't worry," he said as he crested the top of the hill. A village sat at the bottom on the other side, nestled against the shore. "Our capital, Vallania, is right on the shores of the sea. The direct ocean breeze makes the heat far more pleasant than the desert like this, where the air is too still. We'll stay in the village of Oceanmere for the night and then ride along the coast for the rest of our journey. This is the most suffocating of the heat you'll experience."

Thunder struggled to trudge through the deep sands, forcing Etan and me to lean forward over his neck to help him balance on the incline. I felt guilty for the poor creature, but he never complained, and Etan periodically handed him apples and carrots and special treats that seemed to keep him hydrated. He whinnied happily every time he received one of the circular treats that looked like candy.

With a final shove from his rear legs, Thunder crested the top of the dune. A village came into view at the base of the mountain of sand on the other side, nestled into the side of the ocean waters, which glimmered with a color of blue so vivid I never could have imagined it on my own. Even the ocean I'd seen when we'd crossed from Nothrek to Alfheimr hadn't been like this; it had been covered in mist and nearly gray, a moody and mysterious body of water that had quickened my heart rather than calmed it.

Thunder began the descent without hesitating, and our weight shifted to lean back to counteract the change in balance. His steps slid through the sand with practiced ease as the tiny grains rolled down the hill beside him.

The village below was gated, an enormous stone wall surrounding the side of the town that abutted the desert. From our vantage point at the top of the dune, it was hard to guess just how tall the wall might have been. But the homes within were smaller, dwarfed inside by the size of it, and I had to wonder exactly what it was designed to keep out.

Only those who knew of the presence of the village would have any clue it existed with the way the dunes kept it hidden from travelers passing by.

Even this far from the shores, blocked by the buildings and the wall that separated us from them, I felt the cooling sensation of the water on my skin. The humidity from before wasn't stifling, instead coming on a gentle breeze that soothed my sun-kissed skin. The sea was a tangible thing in the air, a promise of relaxation, and some of the tension bled out from my body.

"Have you ever been in the ocean?" Etan asked, and there was a wistful quality to his question. It was clear that he enjoyed time in the water himself, but the only water I'd ever set foot in had been the hot springs in the tunnels where we bathed. It had been warm and calming in its own right, easing sore muscles after Imelda and I trained with some of the others, but it felt different than how I imagined the sea would feel. Refreshingly cool waters on a hot summer's day rather than the warm comfort of a bath.

"Even if I hadn't grown up within the tunnels, the people who came from the surface after the Veil fell said that even touching the sea was forbidden. They weren't permitted to fish from the ocean or set foot upon a boat for fear that the magic of Faerie would poison them," I explained, shrugging my shoulders as I swayed when Thunder stumbled slightly.

"Why would we poison the humans? The war was not something we wanted as a whole. We merely wanted to protect our human mates, who were viewed as abominations after the humans decided they didn't want to worship the Old Gods any longer," Etan said, and he shook his head as if he understood very little of what drove the humans to rebel all those centuries ago. "While I can't fault the humans for wanting to stand on their own feet and resisting the devotion some of the Gods reveled in, they took it too far and sought to eradicate our mates. If they'd only allowed our mates to come to Alfheimr, the war might have been avoided entirely and countless lives saved."

The gate came closer, until I could see the sentries standing guard behind the gate's iron, which must have weakened them just by proximity. I made the mental note to ask Etan what the gate was intended for—what it was meant to keep *out*.

"I think you underestimate what small men are willing to do

when they feel like life handed them cards that made them *less*. Shifting people's allegiance from the Old Gods to the New Gods meant that the Fae were no longer these unattainable beauties that women desired, but predators who fed us lies to manipulate us into subservience. The nobles told humans whatever they needed to in order to earn their devotion for themselves, and they did that by giving us a monster to fear," I said, watching as Etan shifted his reins into one hand and wrapped his other arm around my stomach. As if he needed to feel me there with him, to *feel* that my words were not spoken out of emotion but out of logic and understanding of how something as fragile as history could be rewritten to serve a single man's purpose.

"But the Fae never lied. Your Old Gods *are* the children of the Primordials. If that does not make them Gods, then what does?" Etan asked, and I smiled as I understood his confusion. To him, the Gods were as close as possible to the Primordials that had been responsible for the creation of all the world and the people in it, now that the Primordials had vanished from our world.

"I don't think it is the technicality of the word that matters, in the end. With something as fragile as faith, all that matters is what men believe. What good is being a God, when the people you're meant to rule over believe you to be the villain in their story?" I asked, as he pulled Thunder to a stop before he could reach the gate. "Will it matter to your people if I'm a Goddess or just another Fae? Or will the only thing they see be the fact that I am the daughter of the woman who killed their King? Who killed *their* God?"

Etan was quiet for a moment, his arms tense where they surrounded me. "They are our people, Fallon. Just as much yours as mine, and you need to start thinking of them that way if you want them to respect you. It's true that they'll see you as Mab's daughter at first, but you're also Rheaghan's niece. Your blood doesn't get to define you if you don't let it, especially when there is both good and bad within it."

"I barely knew him," I argued.

"Yet I see far more of him in you than I do of her. You're loyal to a fault, and your choices are made out of love and kindness. You're stubborn as Hel and reluctant to change, but never cruel. You can easily redefine the way our people see you by simply letting them get to know you. It may take some time, but if the nobles can rewrite the history of Nothrek, then you can choose who you want to be in this new life," he said, and I considered those words.

I'd never gotten to choose what I wanted for myself, and part of my desperate desire for freedom stemmed from that. Each lifetime I'd been born, Imelda had brought me back to the tunnels where everyone had a preconceived notion of who and what I was simply for the history that I couldn't escape. In every lifetime, she'd trained me as her apprentice. In every lifetime, I'd been the same. It begged the question, who would I be if given the choice?

I wasn't sure I knew the answer.

Dropping the reins entirely, Etan reached around me to capture my chin between his fingers and turn me to look at him. "Do you still think me your villain, Sunfire? Or has your opinion of me already begun to change? If you can see the truth of who I am this quickly after our rough start, then maybe you should believe our people are capable of that, too," he said, his voice low and tinged with seduction and something dark. Like a promise of games to come, his eyes burned as he stared down at my mouth.

I hesitated, trying to determine how much I wanted to offer him in my response. "I don't think you're a villain, Etan. I think you play one very well, but there's something softer hidden beneath those sharp edges. I don't know if our goals align or if we're going to survive one another, but you're not the man I thought you were."

Etan's slow smile was addictive, transforming the harsher lines of his face into a thing of beauty. "Every time I think I have gotten to the bottom of your depths, you surprise me yet again," he murmured, leaning forward to kiss me briefly. He picked up the reins in the next moment, continuing our walk to the gate without another word.

"It's Etan!" one of the guards yelled to the man who stood beside the wheel to draw up the gate. There were smiles on their faces as Etan guided Thunder into the village and immediately stopped in the center of the courtyard. He dismounted quickly, going to the guards and allowing them to hug him and clap him on the back with a friendly familiarity that would have caught me off guard only two days prior.

"Welcome home," one of the other guards said, but his eyes strayed to me where I remained atop Thunder. I straightened my back, feeling the weighted assessment in that stare, and didn't dare to dismount until Etan told me to. As much as I might not have been able to trust the Fae male with my heart, I knew my safety mattered to him and that was something I could rely on in these situations where I knew no one.

The guards couldn't have possibly known who I was, so I hoped the appraising look was because my hair was probably a mess from our journey. "Who have you brought us?" the guard asked Etan with a curious look in his eye and a raised brow.

Another guard smacked the one who had spoken, nodding to me respectfully as Etan grinned and made his way back to Thunder. Reaching up, he gripped me around the waist and waited for my subtle nod of permission before he plucked me off the horse and brought me to stand beside him. "This is Rheaghan's niece, Fallon. We're to be married as soon as we return to Vallania."

I didn't miss the careful phrasing of my introduction, reframing my heritage to serve our purpose best.

"The lost Princess?" the guard asked, bowing his head in respect, though there was a certain skepticism in his expression. I couldn't blame him, given who that meant my mother was.

"Yes. Fallon was once called Maeve. Hopefully you will not judge her for the proximity to her mother any more than you did Rheaghan," Etan said, the words scolding, but he lessened the sting by reaching out and resting his hand on the other man's shoulder. "Give her a chance, and she'll prove to be more like him than you could ever imagine. But first, I need to take her to the sea."

He took my hand in his, guiding me through the village streets. The buildings had been made out of warm-toned clay, the two-to three-story structures surrounding us as we walked the streets. The wall and gate behind us must have been at least five stories tall.

The ground beneath my feet was a different kind of sand than we'd encountered in the desert, tan in color instead of the red earth that had made me stumble. This sand was packed down to form streets that were lined with people selling goods from stands. They smiled as we passed, greeting Etan by name in a way that I would have expected for Rheaghan. Reverence laced every word they spoke, but it also came with a familiarity that accentuated the way he greeted each and every person by name.

I wondered just how far Etan's deception went, if the court at Tar Mesa and Mab's loyal followers were the only ones who did not know that he wasn't as loyal as he seemed. These people did more than just honor him as their King's second-in-command, and the one who was likely to fill the role as their ruler now that he had passed, but I couldn't help but wonder how they kept that secret from Mab.

Did they know that Rheaghan was gone? I swallowed at the thought of Etan having to be the one to inform them of the loss. It made a little of my excitement for the ocean sink deep in my gut with dread. But Etan's energy was potent, his broad smile as we emerged from the streets and stumbled onto the open sands of the shore pulsing off him in waves. He pulled me down to the water, kicking off his boots with a laugh as I did the same. He released me long enough to let me get them off without falling on my face, taking my hand once again when I was done and ignoring my hesitation. There were giant boulders within the water, huge rocks that jutted out from the turquoise depths as Etan's feet splashed in the shallow tide.

I sucked back a breath as the refreshing water lapped at my feet, gathering my dress up in my hands to avoid getting it wet. Shells adorned the sand at my feet, whole and intact in all shapes and sizes, as Etan pulled me closer to him. His stomach touched my chest, his smile overjoyed as he reached down and scooped me into his arms. I lost sight of the shells as he turned me, and I had to crane my neck to keep my stare on the water instead of the sun burning bright in the sky above.

Squealing as Etan carried me farther out to sea, I looked back toward the shore to watch a crowd of Sidhe gather to watch us. The smiles on their faces were playful, matching the mischievous grin I found on Etan's face when I turned back to look at him.

"Etan, don't you dare!" I screamed as the water lapped around my back as he strode deeper, sending a chill through my middle as it touched my belly.

With a deepening grin, Etan leaned down to kiss my forehead. "Don't I dare do what, Sunfire?" he asked, his suspicious smile confirming everything for the brief moment before he tossed me into the water.

I held my breath, sinking below the surface with my eyes open. The salt stung, but I couldn't make myself close them as I took in the fish swimming all around us in every color imaginable. Holding my breath, I stayed beneath the water as long as I could before I touched my feet to the bottom and stood, and then I surfaced, sucking back a lungful of air and flinging my hair back out of my face.

"I am going to kill you while you sleep," I sputtered, my warning doing nothing to dissuade him as he swam farther out. I didn't dare with the dress I wore, knowing it would be entirely possible for my legs to get tangled up in it and have it weigh me down. I hadn't done much swimming in the spring in the tunnels, mostly using it to get clean or seek out a partner or two when I wanted pleasure.

"I can think of no better way to go than having your face be the last thing I see and drifting off only to never wake," he said teasingly as he swam back toward me. Taking my hand in his, he guided me back to the sandy shore and the Sidhe who waited there. Some had moved into the water, dressed in clothing that looked like it was intended for swimming. I'd never seen anything like it before, and children frolicked and danced on the sand, playing in the shallow water as we walked out of the ocean.

"Hello, Etan!" a young girl said, grabbing him by his other hand and tugging him to dance with her. He spun her with a flourish as a handful of Sidhe and Lliadhe played music on the edge of the beach. I watched, standing alone and not knowing the steps to the dances that they all did, until another girl took pity on me and came up to me, pointing to my head.

"I like your braids! Can you do mine?" Smiling, I nodded, sitting on the sand and having her lower to the ground in front of me so that I could braid the hair back from one side of her face. Someone brought me a cup filled to the brim with wine, and after a nod of approval from Etan, I took my first sip and sighed in contentment.

I watched Etan with his people as I worked and drank, listening to the little girl chatter about how her mother wasn't very good with braids, and she *always* had to wear her hair down, my mouth twisted into a smile the entire time. The sun started to set on the horizon, but in spite of the fading light, the mood and festivities on the beach continued like there wasn't a care in their world.

There was lightness here, a contrast to the darkness of the tunnels and Tar Mesa that went much further than just the sun shining down on us. It seemed so strange to sit in the knowledge that these people had peace like this, when people in Tar Mesa and Nothrek were fighting for their lives every day.

I sat in that, letting that peace wash over me as girl after girl took a seat in front of me and chattered while I braided. I could only hope that one day, I'd find a peace like this for myself.

Eighteen

ETAN

Fallon stumbled as I guided her to the room at the top of the stairs, her drunken giggle warming my insides in a way that was entirely different from the Faerie wine. The manor was large, abutting the sea, so I heard the waves crashing against the shore as I paused and held her still with one arm so she wouldn't fall on her ass. Turning the knob, I guided her into the room we would share for the night before making our way to the sanctuary the next day.

Setting her on the side of the bed, I pointed a finger in her face in an attempt to be serious, though I couldn't help my smile when she gave me a crooked, loopy grin. "Stay," I ordered, unable to control my chuckle when she swayed, lunging toward me to nip at my finger playfully and nearly throwing herself face-first off the bed.

She'd clearly had far more wine than her tolerance could handle. I hadn't anticipated just how sensitive she would be to the stuff until it was too late, and she'd taken to dancing with the women of

Oceanmere—laughing hysterically every time she tripped over her own feet.

I left her sitting, moving to the edge of the room to throw open the curtains, allowing the salty air to penetrate the room. Having spent too much time confined in the stark stillness of Tar Mesa, I craved the life of the summer air on my skin even as I slept. The moon illuminated the edge of the room, the wall entirely open between two supporting pillars so that I could watch the light play over the water and feel the breeze on my face. It was the same room I stayed in every time I visited the seaside village, and while I knew it wasn't mine and other guests frequented it, it felt like a home away from home in many ways.

Fallon stood, stripping off her dress, which had long since dried and stiffened from the salt water when we'd gone for our impromptu swim. Sand covered the fabric as she shoved it down her body, and I only had a moment to think before she was nude before me. She gave me no time to react before she tripped and giggled at her own clumsiness. Stepping out of her dress, she moved to the stone bath that had been hollowed out from the floor at the edge of the room.

The water had already been prepared for us by the staff, and Fallon eased her body down into it with a sigh of contentment. I sighed, following suit and stripping out of the clothes I'd worn in Tar Mesa. If I could have trusted her not to drown in the bath, I likely would have done myself the favor of leaving her to bathe in private rather than subjecting myself to her nudity when I couldn't have her.

My clothes were as stiff and covered in sand as hers when I kicked them aside to be forgotten. The household staff would wash them and place them in the wardrobe to be kept for us until the next time we passed through. We would need more traditional Summer Court clothing as we continued on our journey anyway, allowing our clothing and the sea air to ease the heat and make us more comfortable for the duration.

I joined Fallon in the bath, where she relaxed, her head bent back to rest on the edge so that she looked as if only a moment away from falling asleep as predicted. She adjusted her body as I stepped in across from her and lowered myself to the seat carved into the stone before she could look my way and get an eyeful of my nudity. The room was barely lit, and she brushed her legs against mine, her foot trailing a teasing path along the side of my thigh that I fought to ignore. The suggestive touch made my cock harden against my will, but I refused to act on my arousal for the first time when Fallon was drunk.

The enormous bed across from the bath was low to the ground and big enough to fit a crowd, offering a casual ease to the space that was barren of all else. An open door at the corner led to a space where clothes were stored, but I knew well enough that this room was meant only for sleep, relaxation, and pleasure.

Fallon seemed to have the latter on her mind as she straightened her neck to meet my eye, gliding her hands over the edge of the stone bath. Her legs spread as she sat up, her hands moving to rest atop my knees. Bending her knees, she rested them over my legs where they'd been spread just enough to accommodate her body between them. The position put her on display, and if I dared to look beneath the water, I knew I would see the parts of my future wife that I'd only dreamt of until now.

"Fallon," I warned, resisting the temptation to so much as glance. She smirked in response, fully committed to her seduction as her fingers trailed teasing touches over my knees and rounded to my lower thigh.

"What's wrong, my King? You don't want to play with me?" she asked, her words slow and punctuated as she tried to get them out without slurring.

"You're drunk," I said, believing that to be explanation enough as to why I wouldn't wish to follow this path. Even if the thought of bending her over the edge of the bath and fucking her while the water sloshed around us did already have me hard and ready.

"And?" she asked, giggling as she moved closer to me. Her ass sat between my knees, the warmth of her body so close to where I needed it that I gritted my teeth. I could practically feel her already, and the knowledge that the slightest shift from me would put me inside her tested every bit of control I possessed.

"And the first time I'm inside you will not be when I need to question if you'll even remember it come morning, let alone whether or not you'll come to regret it," I said, leaning forward to tuck her damp hair behind her ear to lessen the sting of the rejection. Even if I was doing the right thing, I didn't want it to hurt her. "The first time I fuck you, I will do so content in the knowledge that you're doing so because you want *me*, not just because you want an orgasm." Even in her drunken haze, Fallon seemed to feel the sting of the words as she flinched back with a pout.

"Who says I don't want you?" she asked, raising her hands from my knees and wringing them in front of her. The move was so vulnerable that I wondered if maybe she wasn't as drunk as I thought, but the hiccup and giggle she released immediately after all but settled that moment of doubt.

"If it's truly me you want and not just a wine-induced need to fuck, I'll still be here when you're sober in the morning. You can have me then, Sunfire," I laughed.

Fallon's gaze fell to the side, staring off at the bed in a way that I suspected she wasn't really seeing it before her. She was lost in her head and to her thoughts, and I gave her the moment to try to gather them enough to speak, even though the exercise in patience pained me. I wasn't sure if I could trust whatever she said to me while she'd been drinking, but some part of me suspected that maybe, just maybe, it would release her inhibitions and her hesitations enough for her to let me in.

Just a little.

"Not wanting you is not the problem, Etan. It's everything that comes along with you that worries me," she said, her voice quiet. "I worry I won't be a good wife or queen. That my need to feel all the things they kept from me in those tunnels will prevent me from being what you and the rest of the Summer Court need. I want to be selfish for once. I don't want to have to choose." The words were tossed out in a way that I knew wasn't entirely like her. The openness and honesty of that insecurity hung between us, pulsing back and forth as she swallowed and the wine took over.

"Fallon," I said, my voice softening as I reached between us and caught her hands in mine. No matter the cause of the word vomit and the horrified expression on her face as she realized what she'd said, I knew that the words and the emotion behind them was genuine. "Nobody is going to lock you away in Vallania. You don't have to choose."

"But I'll be your wife," she said, her brow furrowing in confusion. "Doesn't that mean that outside of whatever trips we take for politics, you'll shut me away and expect me to run your household or bear children—" She broke off, seeming to realize the impossibility of children for us.

We weren't mates, and that meant I would never have a little girl with Fallon's hazel eyes or a boy with her shrewd intelligence. After spending hours watching her braid hair for the girls of Oceanmere and the way they flocked to her, that truth was heavy in my chest. "We will not have children for you to bear or raise, Sunfire. It will be just you and me, forever."

"And the entire court that's depending on us," she said, her words feeling heavy as I smiled.

"I think you will find that the Summer Court is generally home to some of the most spontaneous of the Fae. We're an impulsive group, and our people would not judge us if we take off for destinations unknown every so often. I promise I will take you to explore Alfheimr if that is what you want. It is never going to be my goal to lock you away like a queen in a tower," I said, reassuring her once again of my intentions for our relationship. I couldn't fault her for the distrust given how she'd lived for so long.

I barely understood anything about what had come to pass in Nothrek in the time since the Veil had been erected, but what I did know was that it had left a lasting mark on Fallon. Given that she'd been hidden away from the worst of it, I couldn't imagine what the other women who came to Alfheimr would be battling with their mates.

Having love that was predestined was a blessing in some ways and a curse in others.

Estrella's blatant defiance made more sense now that I understood. She had spent lifetimes in subservience. She refused to spend another, and the understanding I'd gleaned from Fallon's assertions about Nothrek endeared her to me a little more. I didn't like what her recklessness could bring to those around her, including Fallon, but I couldn't fault her for it either.

"You would be smarter to lock me away, and we both know it," Fallon said, scoffing with disbelief. "I don't know the first thing about what it takes to be Fae! I don't even know how to use my magic or what is the norm for any situation I might encounter. I'm going to make a fool of myself, because I've got no clue what is expected of me as Queen," she added, and I filed away the admission she'd given. The slip of words that acknowledged the magic that she carried within her but kept tucked away. Even though I'd suspected it, it was still a shock to my system.

Curiosity burned within me, making me want nothing more than to ask—to demand to know what magic she possessed.

It could be nearly anything.

Instead, I squeezed her hands, leaning forward to kiss her gently enough to silence her protests. Her magic would be there come morning, but the spiral of her thoughts needed handling in that moment. "I was never meant to be King either. We will learn and adapt, and we will do it together. Who cares what's expected of us? We'll do it our way."

"Our way?" she asked, as if the thought hadn't occurred to her that we could simply forge our own path. There was little in the way of traditions when it came to ruling that were passed down from one ruler to another, because there had only been two nobles of the Summer Court since its creation.

And Rheaghan had not had a Queen at his side in all his time as King.

"You can be as involved as you want. There are no rules, Fallon," I said, even though I had every intention of encouraging her to sit at my side in all ways. I touched my mouth to hers once more before backing away slightly, not wanting the energy between us to shift into something sexual all over again.

She nodded slowly, her breath a slow sigh as she considered her options. "No rules," she said, and I had the distinct feeling that there had never been a time when she wasn't controlled in all aspects of her life.

That she'd lived with more rules than she knew how to count.

I resolved to remove them all from our lives, so that she was beholden to none but herself.

Nineteen

FALLON

I woke the next morning clad in a man's tunic, my memories from the night before not as hazy as I would have liked under the circumstances. The way I'd all but thrown myself at Etan made me wince, even as his deep, even breaths ruffled my hair where he'd cuddled into me as we slept.

"I wish we could stay here for a few days," he said, confirming that he'd awoken before I did, and stayed to avoid disturbing me.

I pulled away and sat, tugging my knees into my chest and feeling vulnerable after last night. I didn't feel hungover in the sense that I would have expected, given how much wine I'd drunk the night before, but my head felt groggy as Etan brushed my hair out of my face and moved to sit beside me.

"You want to go frolic in the ocean some more?" I teased, smiling through my discomfort. The compromise we'd reached the night before left me feeling raw, because while I'd had physical intimacy, I'd never had the emotional intimacy that came with a relationship. The latter left me more exposed and laid bare than sex ever had.

"Fuck the ocean," Etan said with a grin. "I meant I want to stay in this room with you so we can have time to ourselves. I think it would benefit both of us to lay the foundations of our relationship before we tackle all the other stuff that's waiting for us at home. If only we had the time to spare."

His smile was gentle, as if he understood just how deeply the promise of the duty that waited for us would affect me. "What exactly will it entail?" I asked, curling my legs even tighter to my chest.

Etan adjusted his position, moving farther onto the bed and pulling me into his lap. He wore nothing but a pair of shorts, leaving his broad chest naked for me to take in the curve of his shoulders and the grooved muscles that covered his torso. Even though we were both barely clothed, the position wasn't intended to be sexual as his hands came down on my waist and squeezed reassuringly. I hated to admit that I appreciated the closeness of his body, that his skin beneath my hands did something to soothe me.

"We will prepare for the wedding and coronation separately. You with the women of the court and me with the men. They'll prepare you according to our customs and we'll be married at sunset. We will celebrate all night and then we will consummate our marriage in the tides before the court as the sun rises over the horizon. I trust the audience will not bother you," he said with a little smirk. My cheeks flushed even though his words were true, because I was *very* comfortable with being watched.

Enjoyed it, even.

"They'll each offer a sliver of their immortality to us through touch as we make love. The men making the offering to you and the women to me," he said, and my brow snapped down.

"They'll touch you?" The venom in the words shocked even me, because I'd never come close to feeling possessive over a man, not even once.

Fuck.

Etan grinned. "Not like that. It's a brush of a hand over your shoulder or arm or something mostly innocent enough outside of the context of the situation. It's a touch that even mates can tolerate."

"You mean the context where you are buried inside of me at that moment?" I asked, offering a bitter smile that didn't reach my eyes.

"I like you jealous, Sunfire," he said, reaching lower to grip my ass in his hands. My core tightened in response, part of me hoping he would take it a step further and do something with the hardening flesh between his legs.

Instead, he gave it a squeeze before he lifted me from his lap and set me on the bed, standing to go to the doorway at the corner of the room. He returned with new clothes, depositing them on the bed before lifting the brush in his hands and taking his place behind me. He was gentle as he used it to untangle what had to be a horrible mess after I'd slept with it wet from our bath.

Grumbling beneath my breath, I attempted not to display my discomfort with my own emotions as he finished up and we dressed, then made our way out of the manor and to Thunder.

When we were finally settled and had exited the gates of Oceanmere, I finally dared to broach the subject I'd been trying to avoid. "I'm sorry for my word vomit last night. I wasn't entirely in control of my mouth."

"Don't be sorry, Fallon," Etan said gently from his place behind me. The impending nuptials waited for us there, and I desperately wanted to undo the agreement we'd reached the night before. Etan didn't deserve my back-and-forth on my feelings, or to feel the brunt of my nerves directed at him when they really had very little to do with him. "But try to remember there are two sides to every coin. Becoming queen will come with a burden of responsibility, but it also means that there are few who can tell you what to do. You have the power to make a difference as queen. What power do you really have if you spend your life wandering and at the whims of Alfheimr wherever you go?"

I hated that the thought had promise, that the very idea of helping others appealed to my human nature. I hadn't been able to save Estrella from Tartarus, but maybe I could help create a better world for her if she returned.

"As true as that might be, I didn't need to burden you with all of my insecurities. Those are mine to work through and you have enough to worry about with Rheaghan's death and having to step up for the Summer Court," I said, wincing when I realized I was rambling all over again in my nervousness.

"We're partners, Fallon. That means your insecurities and worries are mine to bear, just as mine are yours. We cannot do this together if we aren't honest with one another," he said, letting me settle into silence as I thought through his words.

Leaving Oceanmere was more difficult than I'd expected when we'd arrived the night prior. The desire to stay and explore the town, get to know the people I'd only had the chance to meet in passing, was nearly overwhelming. I'd never really imagined myself desiring to put down roots anywhere, always dreaming of being on the move and never having someone to tell me to sit still.

But if I had wanted to settle in one place for a while, I had a feeling it would have been a place like this. Even though the village was small, it felt endless with the way the sea abutted it. It made me wonder what was beyond it, if Nothrek existed far off the shores or if we were on the other side of Alfheimr.

Were we really alone in the world, or was there more out there just waiting to be explored?

"You're quiet," Etan observed as he guided me to Thunder, saying goodbye to each and every person we passed.

"Just thinking about what might be out there, and who they might be if there are more people in the world than we know," I said, turning my stare up to Etan. He nodded as if he understood, but didn't respond in any way that indicated he might have greater knowledge than I did.

"There could be. Some Fae have sailed to explore, but they never last more than a few days. It is difficult to be separated from Alfheimr for too long, and I think only the call of a mate bond could force someone to bear that discomfort long enough to truly discover what might be out there," he mused. I appreciated that he didn't treat me like it was stupid to wonder, instead smiling at me softly.

He promised a male who approached us that we would return soon, and that when we did we would stay for a couple days and not a single night. The men clapped him on the back as if they trusted his word to return implicitly, not a single doubt in their expressions as they turned gentle smiles to me.

The mother of that first girl who'd asked me to braid her hair, Iulia, approached as Etan bid his farewells, her daughter at her side until she moved to wrap her arms around my legs and squeeze in a tight hug.

"Maybe the next time you return, you can teach me how to braid properly so that I can be responsible for the smile on her face," her mother said, a broad grin accompanying the shake of her head. Her blond hair cascaded over her shoulders and gleamed in the sunlight, her features open and warm just like her daughter's had been.

"I'd be happy to teach both of you," I said, casting a raised brow down at the little girl who'd made me feel welcome in a strange place. "Etan has promised it won't be long before we return. I'd love it if you could give me a tour of your village when we do."

"I can show you my house, and the school, and where Mommy works!" Iulia said, her smile infectious as her mother touched a hand to her shoulder and pulled her back from me. The touch was gentle and easy, tucking her daughter into her as Etan reappeared at my side and stole my attention.

"Livia. I trust all has been quiet the last few weeks," he said, greeting the mother by name.

She nodded her head forward, the interaction easy and casual. "As it always is in our little haven," she said as a male came up behind her. He was handsome, with blond hair that matched the rest of his family's, but there was something that came with a stark realization as I followed the cut of that blond hair to the red *viniculum* at his neck.

He was human. His ears were not pointed, but shaped the same as the ones I'd grown up seeing on everyone in the tunnels. He smiled as if he knew the path of my thoughts, rubbing a hand over the back of his neck. "I take it I am the first human mate you've seen since coming to Alfheimr?" he asked, and I flushed as I looked around me.

There weren't a ton of them, but as soon as I looked closely enough, I saw the reality of the handful of humans who filled the courtyard alongside the Sidhe they accompanied.

"I'm so sorry. I didn't mean to stare," I said, shaking my head. It should have stood to reason that the humans would be present, that they'd have survived if they completed the bond, because they lived as long as their mate.

There were children here, and given that mate bonds were rarely between two Fae, it had been foolish not to realize that meant humans were present.

"It's alright," he said, placing his hand on top of his daughter's head. "It's been centuries, but I can still remember how strange it was when I first came to Alfheimr. It's jarring when you first realize how little differences there actually are between us."

"So much so that you cannot even tell unless you look very deeply," I said with a laugh. I knew there was more to it—knew that the inability to tell them apart was partly due to the bond itself and the power it lent to the human. The Fae Marked moved differently than they had when they were entirely human, with agility and strength that they never could have dreamed of before. There was no sickness or injury they could not heal, and it took a great deal more to exhaust them.

He reached forward, taking my hands in his. Etan eyed the contact and ground his teeth together but said nothing. "You aren't alone here. I understand your circumstances are unique, but your upbringing was more similar to the rest of us who were once human than it was to any of the other Fae who will see themselves as your peers. Those of us who understand the transitions you're experiencing are here, if only you're willing to seek us out when the differences between our worlds become too much for you."

I nodded, swallowing past the burn in my throat. He looked at me with such understanding, a sympathy that I hadn't expected to find in the warmth of his brown-eyed stare. When was the last time I'd felt truly understood? Like someone knew exactly how jarring the reality of all these new people and creatures and places that I never could have even imagined could be on my soul? I wanted to explore, but I wanted to see the beauty in Alfheimr.

Instead, I'd been plunged into the horrors of it.

"Thank you," I said, feeling the weight of Etan's heavy stare on the side of my face. When the human released me, Etan was quick to fill the void and take my hand in his. His warmth was so much stronger than that of the man who'd touched me, as if the sun itself burned beneath his skin. He guided me toward Thunder without another word, severing the connection that only worsened the desire I felt to remain in the seaside village.

Perhaps it was my dread over what was to come and what waited for us beyond the walls that kept this place so protected from outside influences.

As Etan offered me a leg up so that I could mount Thunder, I settled into the front of the bareback pad and took his reins in my hand. "What does the wall protect them from?" I asked, my curiosity finally getting the best of me as I swallowed.

Etan accepted a leg up from one of the guards, mounting behind me and settling his groin against my ass, then he reached around me to take control of the reins as he spoke an ominous warning. "Let's hope you never have to find out."

Twenty

FALLON

The sun had nearly set on another day by the time we were even preparing to stop for the night. Etan rode hard, excusing the pace he set under the justification that spending a night with the open desert to our right would be a mistake.

Even Thunder didn't seem to object to the notion of continuing on through the grueling, unforgiving fast walk that must have exhausted him in the heat. The only saving grace to the temperatures was the presence of the sea as we rode at the top of the dune closest to the water, letting the ocean air and breeze cool our skin.

The clothing I'd dressed in that morning had also helped ease some of the worst of the temperatures, the fabric and style far more breathable than the thicker, heavier gowns Mab had favored in Tar Mesa. The off-white linen draped over my shoulders lightly, without sleeves even though it had a hood, hanging loosely across my chest and dipping down to a belt at my waist. It fell out into a loose skirt with slits that went high on the outside of the thighs, allowing me to sit far more comfortably on Thunder than I had previously.

Etan's clothing was tailored from that same light, gauzy fabric. An off-white shirt dipped down at the front of his chest, where he wore several chains around his neck, revealing the curve at the top of his pectoral muscles. His pants were a different color than his tunic, a deep blue, belted at his waist and a few shades darker than the overshirt that covered the tunic, which had a hood that he often used to shield his face when the wind blew the sand up in a particularly violent arc.

Etan pushed Thunder into a trot in spite of the uneven footing as the sky began to change colors on the horizon, the deep red and orange painting the blue in a way that took my breath away. Even that couldn't settle the unease I felt at the cause of Etan's rush; I didn't want to consider what might be hiding in the desert to instill that kind of fear in him.

There'd been minimal discussion of my magic, because we both knew that it was lacking from what had transpired in the Shadow Court. Even with that knowledge, I'd never stopped to ask Etan if he had *any* magic of his own or what his lineage might have been. All I knew was that his parents had dropped him off at the Summer Court and he'd been raised by Primordials.

But that told me nothing of his bloodline or whatever magic might course through his veins. Most of the children of the Gods had none, and that put us at a great disadvantage being out here in the open.

"If it's so dangerous, why didn't we bring your guards?" I hissed, wincing when Thunder curved over the top of a dune and made his way away from the sea. Etan steered him down the bank on the other side, pulling me back into his body behind me to shift my weight and counteract the sudden change in balance.

"It's a journey we have to make alone. Trust me, I didn't make the damn rules," he grunted, nudging Thunder in the side until he picked up a slow canter once we hit the flat plains at the bottom of the dune.

I shut my mouth, deciding I would argue with him about the foolishness of these traditions when we made it somewhere safe to spend the night. We pushed along as the sun began to fade over the horizon, Etan's occasional curses as he looked over his shoulders ratcheting my anxiety ever higher.

"Etan," I started, not knowing what to say. I didn't know what we were looking for or where we were going, but the only thing I saw before us, behind us, and all around us was an endless expanse of desert.

"We're almost there," he grunted, bearing the weight of my body thrashing as he pushed Thunder into an open gallop. The fact that I'd never even seen a horse until recently worked against me, making me completely unable to figure out what to do with my body in this new gait. Etan held me still as I winced, my eyes catching sight of something in the distance to our left.

"What the fuck is that?" I asked, my voice barely a whisper even though the words felt shrill. It was as if my eyes couldn't connect with what I was seeing, the red mass a mirage in the distance. I couldn't tell if it was a trick of light or the wind manipulating the sand into a shape, and I squinted to see better.

"Fuck!" Etan hissed, pulling to the right on Thunder's reins. The horse obeyed with a quiet whinny.

The red mass *moved*, surging forward in a motion that felt oddly reminiscent of the way Thunder's gallop felt beneath me. That same rear-charged motion propelled the thing forward, and it closed the gap between us with an unnatural speed that Thunder's exhausted form couldn't outpace.

I looked over Etan's shoulder, my eyes widening when I realized exactly why the motion seemed so much like Thunder's. The figure was a horse and rider, a skinless monstrosity of red muscle and sinew. Tiny flames burned in the place of both the horse's and rider's eyes, erupting from its mouth. Where blood might have flowed through veins was only lines of fire, and I shuddered as the pair gained on us.

The rider didn't have any legs of his own, the two somehow melded together with flesh alone so that they were one being. The rider had no hair or clothing, the inner working of the human body flexing with every movement. He was faceless, with only those burning eyes to add any definition to his person. In his hands was a long staff, the sharp blade already coated in blood.

"Oh my Gods," I mumbled, turning to face the front and trying to focus on mirroring Etan's body movements in the hope that it would help Thunder run faster. The sand beneath our feet began to change, shifting to more of the brown dirt that I'd seen in Nothrek. Soon the dirt was filled with blades of grass, the area ahead of us teeming with life. A copse of trees rose up in the distance like a mirage, mountains surrounding the wooded area as if to shelter it. Streams of water trailed down the mountainsides, cascading over cliffs to form waterfalls that drifted into the valley below as our path curved downward. The sound was as raucous as thunder filling the air, only contrasted by the creature following us and gaining on us.

"We aren't going to make it," Etan said, forcing my hands to wrap around the reins. He released them entirely, turning to the rear so he could swing his leg over Thunder's butt and face the creature as it caught up with us. "Aim for the woods. You'll be safe there. The Nuckelavee won't risk the Gods' wrath by wandering into their sanctuary, even for a meal. Stay until morning and then follow the coast south to Vallania."

I flinched, spinning back to look at him in shock as he vaulted off Thunder and rolled to his feet. He pulled the sword from the scabbard strapped to his back, preparing himself to fight off the creature he'd called a Nuckelavee.

"I'm not going to leave you," I snapped, pulling on the reins to get Thunder to slow.

"Yes, you fucking are, Sunfire. Go!" He tossed dirt at Thunder, making the horse rear slightly before he took off in the direction of the sanctuary. I watched Etan, trusting Thunder to know the way to safety as the Nuckelavee reached him. His spear met Etan's sword with the clash of metal.

I dropped the reins entirely, frantically searching through the packs strapped over Thunder's withers and rear for a weapon that I might use. My hands found leather, and I pulled the pack of throwing daggers free with a grin. Taking the first in my right hand, I grabbed the reins with my left and pulled Thunder to turn around, heading back in Etan's direction as I kept the throwing knife pinned to my side to maintain the element of surprise.

"Fallon!" Etan shouted, rage coating his voice as he swung for the legs of the creature that charged him. It jumped over his sword, sweeping the spear back and cutting across Etan's arm with a skill that horrified me.

It was toying with him.

I flung the knife, watching with glee when it sank into the shoulder of what would have been a person under any other circumstances. The horse neighed in protest, revealing a sharp set of teeth that would have looked more at home on a wolf than a horse, but with no mouth to speak, the rider was silent.

I curved Thunder around in a wide circle as the creature faced me and came to a stop, slowly pulling the knife free from his shoulder and tossing it to the sand at its feet. Blood trickled down the creature's leg, and my gaze dropped to the wound where its chest curved into its belly. I couldn't say if it had been a blow Etan landed or a previous injury, but I grabbed the biggest knife from the pack and shoved the rest into the saddlebag.

Kicking at Thunder's sides, I encouraged him to run away from the creature, to lure it away from Etan and head toward the sanctuary. The creature followed, leaving me to heave a deep breath as I patted the side of Thunder's neck.

I had no clue if the horse could understand or would care, but it brought me some measure of comfort to speak the words and *hope* it would do as I asked.

Adrenaline flooded my veins as I spoke, the feeling both terrifying and addictive. "When I dismount, you run clear and get Etan, okay, handsome?" I said, keeping my voice soft and soothing.

Thunder turned when I pulled on the reins, changing directions suddenly as his feet sank into the uneven ground below. He righted his balance, surging toward the Nuckelavee even though I knew he must feel the same terror I did.

I swallowed as I moved, swinging my leg over Thunder's neck suddenly and leaping from his back. I narrowly avoided the swing of the creature's spear as it swept above the horse part's neck, collapsing to the ground between the horse's legs and sinking my knife into the tiny wound at its chest. It neighed in pain as I dragged the blade down, using the creature's forward momentum against it as it carved through muscle, and a fresh flood of blood spilled down to cover me.

The Nuckelavee stumbled when I finally pulled the knife free, forcing myself to my feet and blinking through the thick coating of blood that covered me. I watched as it sank to its knees in the front, organs hanging loosely from its stomach.

Thunder charged toward me, Etan riding on his back with a furious expression on his face. He held out an arm that I stretched up to reach, letting him grasp me around the elbow and haul me up onto Thunder's back behind him.

We didn't waste any time before turning and racing for the sanctuary, pained howls filling the air behind us as the Nuckelavee fell to its side.

"I'm going to fucking kill you myself," Etan grumbled, turning over his shoulder to look at me with a glare.

I'd have smiled more broadly if I didn't worry I'd get blood in my mouth.

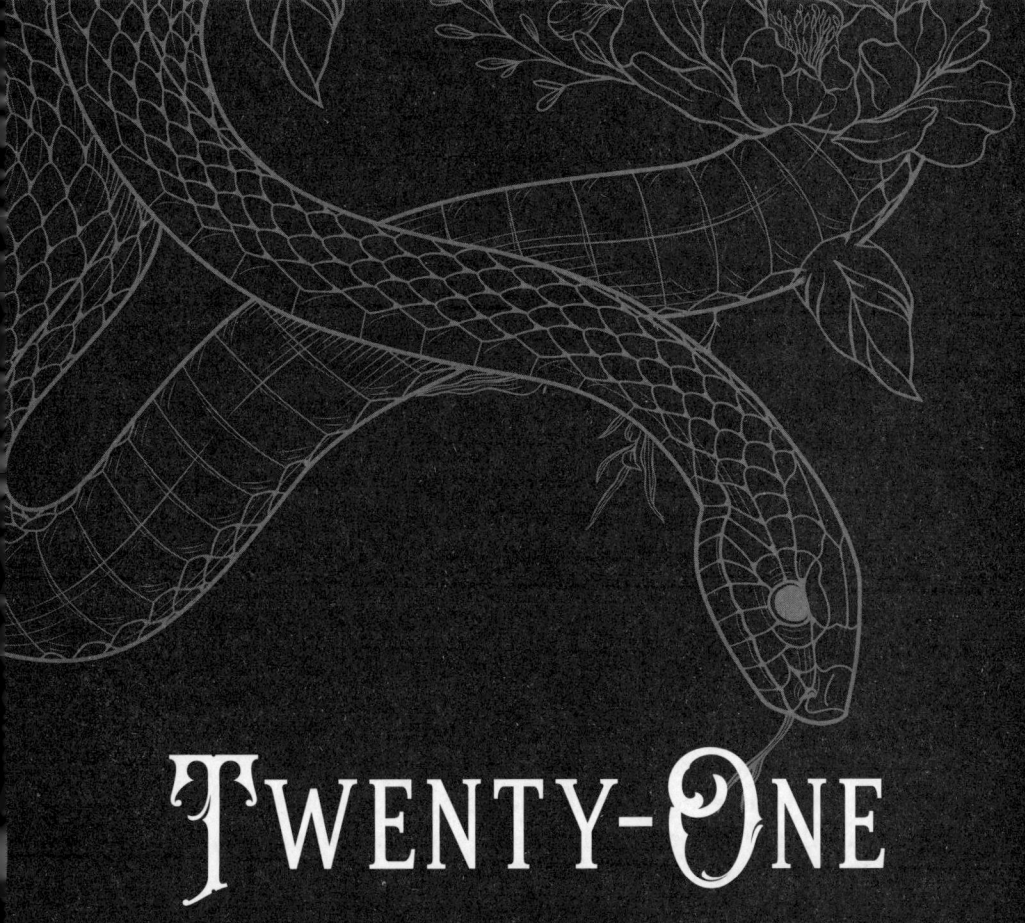

Twenty-One

FALLON

The air seemed to change as we entered the haven between the mountains, Thunder's step picking up pep as if he too could feel the change surrounding us. I stiffened against Etan's spine as my skin buzzed with the feeling of magic kissing along it, like tiny wisps drifting through the air that I could not see. The Nuckelavee had remained where it had fallen, whether it was dead or merely injured to the point it could no longer follow after us.

The heat became balmy, slicking my skin with sweat until I became acutely aware of the pulsing heat that spread through me. But that heat didn't come from the air entirely, instead forming in my core and forcing me to shift a little uncomfortably.

I hoped Etan didn't notice the strange sensation occurring within me, the oddly timed arousal that I had no explanation for. It was far from the first time I'd felt it, having had my share of partners in the tunnels of the Resistance. Our public baths and limited opportunities for entertainment meant that few were unaware of the pleasures to be found in the comfort of another's body.

"What is this place?" I asked, trying to refocus my attention on my surroundings.

"There were four Primordials who once called the Summer Court home," Etan said, his voice sounding lower somehow, deeper than I was used to. I couldn't decide if it was something actually occurring or the haze in my head that made it seem real. "When our court was new, Diell thought we should pay homage to those who had already chosen to leave the public eye. We could no longer see them, but she knew they still existed and that their magic was present around us."

"Fascinating," I said through gritted teeth. I forced my jaw to relax, instead chewing on the inside corner of my mouth.

"She put sanctuaries throughout the court. Places intended for the Fae of her court to go to pay their respects to the Primordials who came before all of us. Many made offerings, and it was said that the size of your offering determined the blessing they gave in return," he explained, continuing on as he guided Thunder down a somewhat narrow pass. It curved around the edge of a mountain, taking us away from the descent into the valley and the vague impression of the capital that I could see now in the distance to the south. I wanted nothing more than to continue on our journey, but I kept quiet as he tugged Thunder to the side of the path, dismounted, and tied his reins to a tree branch. Pulling an apple from the pack slung across the horse's rump, he held it out with an open palm and patted the horse's neck when Thunder took it happily. A bucket of water hung from the branch as if someone had prepared for us, and Etan reached up to grasp me around the waist and pull me down.

I swung my leg over Thunder's rear, sliding down slowly so I didn't disturb his snack. Etan was behind me when I landed, my back dragging over him slowly as I glided to my feet. His broad form left nothing to the imagination, making me entirely too aware of the fact that I was not the only one so inexplicably affected.

He moved away from me finally and took an extra bucket filled with water from the tree, dumping the entirety of it over my head as I sputtered. The water that ran down my skin was tinted with pink as it washed away most of the blood that had not yet had time to dry on me. My clothing would remain stained, leaving me to look like a nightmare made real, but I glared up at him over the method he'd used to clean me.

He only smiled bitterly, his anger at my risking myself still palpable between us. "Don't ever do something that reckless again," he ordered, cupping my cheek in his hand to gentle the words.

"I survived, didn't I?" I asked, grinning at his irritation.

"I have to wonder where you learned to use a knife that well," he said.

"Like I said, I had a lot of free time in the tunnels." I shrugged, wandering away from him to explore the clearing where we stood. "What do Diell's sanctuaries have to do with us?" I asked to bring us back to the pertinent conversation, my own voice sounding far more husky than I could ever recall.

I spun when Etan grabbed hold of my wrist, tugging me back to him. With Thunder's bulky body behind me, they made me feel pinned between two dangerous creatures. Etan hung his head, his brown eyes holding mine and making me feel as if he stared right through me. Like he could see my arousal in the stare that held his, and his tense mouth spread into an arrogant grin. He leaned closer, bending so his mouth was only a breath from mine and his nose brushed alongside mine. "Come with me."

He took my hand in his, guiding me away from Thunder finally and tugging me down the narrow path. It was just wide enough for the two of us to fit side by side, his hand too warm in mine and the calluses of his thumb rough as he rubbed the back of my hand where he gripped me. "Just before she said goodbye to her children, Diell created a place where those who followed in her footsteps could come and make offerings to all the Summer Primordials at once. A place where they were all present, even in their absence," he said, pushing a tree branch out of the path so that I could move without ducking past it. The branches hung over us like a canopy, offering shade from the blazing sun of the desert where we had started our journey. "She said it would be customary for any who wished to sit upon her throne to come and make their offering to those who came before. When it became clear that Diell had no intention of returning to reclaim her court, Rheaghan came here for the first time and made his own offering. It is believed that the greater the offering, the longer you will be allowed to reign."

We continued along the path, and I waited for the moment that we would find an altar, that we would have to slaughter some poor, innocent animal that had been left for us.

"This path has not been traversed in some time. Are you certain the temple still stands?" I asked, glancing at him. It would be just my luck that we had wasted an entire day riding to a place that had fallen into disuse centuries prior.

He smirked, grasping hold of the tree branch that blocked both our paths. He lifted it as he watched my face, undoubtedly seeing the moment I laid eyes upon the sanctuary before me. I glanced at him in surprise, stepping forward on feet that moved of their own accord. Drawn to the magical haven before me, I took in the sight of something that made no sense whatsoever.

The haven was surrounded by trees on all sides, creating a private alcove that no one would ever find by chance. "Only Kings and Queens of Summer and their guests are allowed to step foot in this place," he said, following after me. "Since Rheaghan was unmarried, he often brought companions to share in the experience with him."

Lightning cracked above us, rippling through the daylit sky with the force of a summer storm. The light mist of summer rain fell down around us, rinsing the sweat and remaining blood from my skin as I tipped my head up to feel the moisture on my face. The sun shone bright here, like we were at the peak of day with the sun at its apex, even though it was already dusk outside the sanctuary. Flowers bloomed around the tree line, covering the ground in life and bursts of color as I moved to the baths carved into the earth.

I was no stranger to the concept of a communal bath, but the one in the tunnels had been far less refined work. Made out of necessity rather than from love and devotion. Four statues surrounded the bath, their forms recognizable even from a distance.

Diell, with her crown of gold as she reached up toward the sky, her eyes closed as if she were basking in the daylight.

Oshun, where she knelt at the edge of the sea, her fingers and feet covered in grains of sand, drops of water dripping down her forearm. Her hair was wet, plastered to the side of her face and neck.

Tempest, with a lightning bolt held in his palms, his chest squared as he stood upon a summer rain cloud.

Gerwyn, with her feathered wings spread out behind her, a smile on her face as she watched a couple embrace.

The four Primordials of the Summer Court sat around the small, circular bath, which was far more intimate than the one I'd spent time in since becoming an adult. "What exactly does this *offering* entail?" I asked, everything in me going still as Etan's hands went to the laces of his tunic. He stepped away from me as he untied them slowly. He reached over his head, grabbing the back of the shirt and tugging it over his head in that distinctly masculine move that I'd never been able to master. His torso was broad, his chest and abs defined. His Fae Marks curled over his collarbone and onto the left side of his chest, swirling lines of red that served as the reminder that no matter what marriage said, he would never really be mine.

There was no mate bond between us, only the simmering attraction between a man and a woman who found one another desirable on a physical level. My soul did not reach out to his as I stared at him, didn't crave him in the way I both feared and hoped would never happen for me.

"That, Sunfire, is up to you. This is the part of this marriage where *we* have control, where Mab cannot dictate who or how we rule," he said, drawing my attention back to his face. "Every court functions a little differently. The magic flows in ways that were determined by the Primordials that brought that magic into existence and made it a tangible thing. Diell and the others chose this place for their transfer of power, where others value family bonds above all else. Only one of us needs to enter the bath, but according to Summer Court tradition, only those who have offered and been accepted, and have been given the blessing of the Primordials in return, can sit upon the throne of the Summer Court."

"If I do not get into the water, I won't be your wife?" I asked, trying to keep my voice neutral. It was such an unexpected turn of events that I couldn't be sure I'd managed it, that the lilt of hope hadn't snuck into my voice. Etan might not have treated me poorly, aside from kidnapping me against my wishes anyway, but that didn't mean I desired to tie myself to him without really knowing him that well. I hadn't had time yet to see if he kept his promises, or if they were empty entirely.

"You'll still be my wife. It's the only way Mab will be satisfied, but she is very aware of this tradition. She knows as well as I do that I cannot force you into this water. You have to enter of your own free will," he explained, dropping his gaze to the surface, which shimmered in the sunlight. "But if you do not enter, you will not be Queen of the Summer Court. Not unless we come back one day so that you can offer yourself when you're ready."

"You would do that? Allow me to change my mind and rule alongside you, after rejecting the notion today?" I asked, leaving off the part where I would be rejecting *him* as well. Though he did not speak of it, I had the feeling that this was the precipice where we determined the type of marriage we would have. While we may not be a love match or fated mates, we still had choices as to how we continued on our path. We could live entirely separate lives, with me as the estranged wife of the Summer King.

Or we could undertake this endeavor together as partners, as temporary as it may be, and embrace our marriage to the full extent of its capabilities.

"That depends on how much you piss me off in the meantime, but yes. I have no desire to take away your choice in this, Sunfire. I want you to choose," he said, crossing his arms over his chest with a smirk. He curled a brow, glancing toward the water. I followed his gaze, staring into the slow current that seemed to keep the water moving, like it ran somewhere in spite of being an isolated pool.

"That's a no, then," I laughed. "What happens if I decide I want to be Queen? Am I required to share your bed?"

His eyes heated as he stared at me, keeping his distance even though I suspected he wanted to close it. "I won't require you to fuck me if you aren't interested, Fallon," he said, that heated stare drifting down my body. "But I am certain this attraction is not one-sided. Should you decide to rule alongside me, I would ask that you be monogamous to me as your husband, whether you are in my bed or not."

"And you? Will you fuck around while expecting me to remain celibate?" The venom in my voice shocked me. I'd never understood why women from Nothrek were upset when their husbands slept with other women—most of them didn't desire their husbands anyway. Why be upset when it meant he left you alone?

Etan grinned, as if the show of jealousy pleased him. "No. So long as I expect monogamy from you, I will return it. I do intend to spend every waking moment buried within my *wife* either way. She just may make me work for it."

I smiled, chewing on the corner of my mouth as I tugged at the laces at the back of my dress. It loosened around my chest, hanging lower in the front to reveal more of my cleavage as I paused.

"There is one thing you should know before you enter the water, Sunfire. To step into the bath is to give yourself over to the Primordials. You will no longer be in control of your body until they're done with us," he said, giving me pause.

"What do you mean I won't be in control?" I asked, tipping my head to the side.

"The Primordials will be in control. We will do as they see fit until they have taken their offering and are willing to give their blessing for our sacrifice. If you get in the water, you must do so with the knowledge that anything could happen, but the most likely outcome will end with me inside of you," he said, smiling as if thinking of stories he'd heard from Rheaghan. "Repeatedly."

The idea of losing my control with Etan didn't bother me as much as it should. Sex was the easiest and simplest part of making this decision. What made me nervous was all the unknowns, the wondering about what else the decision might affect within me, but ultimately I made the choice to take that leap of faith anyway.

The alternative would mean I was subordinate to my husband, and I wanted to be his fucking equal.

I shrugged, backing toward the pool as I slid the straps of my dress down over my shoulders. The dress gathered at my feet, leaving me bare before Etan. His eyes on me didn't bother me in the slightest; I'd gotten used to being seen naked in my time with the rebellion. "I guess it's a good thing I don't have to like you to fuck you, then."

Twenty-Two

ETAN

She glided down the stairs smoothly after stripping off her shoes, the water shimmering and glowing in a halo around her as she trailed her hands through it at her sides. Her back was to me, her face hidden away as my eyes drank in the sight of her fair skin, of the contrast of her raven-black hair as it swept down her spine to touch the surface of the water. The swell of her ass disappeared beneath the haze of the surface, and she didn't stop until she was waist-deep. Her body went still for a moment, waiting, as if the Primordials themselves wanted to know if I would leave her to be ridden by their magic alone, or if I would join her in seeking their blessing.

I hurried to shuck off my pants and boots, starting the journey down the steps with far less grace than Fallon had managed. I came up behind her, the coolness of the refreshing water gliding along my skin as I raised a hand and watched it slide off my body. The water dropped to the surface, the sound of the splash far too loud in the quiet of the bath. Fallon whirled on me the moment my hand rested on her shoulder, her eyes filled with gold. Something eternal stared back at me from within her beautiful face, and it almost pained me that my first moment with her, our first time exposed like this, would come when we would watch ourselves like spectators.

When we would be privy to every action, feel the pleasure of our touch upon one another, but know that we were not alone.

She touched her hand to my cheek, cupping it as she stepped closer to me, allowing the press of her skin against mine. I shuddered, taking in the lines of her face as she pressed onto her toes and touched her mouth to mine.

My senses exploded into the taste of her, into the scent of an ocean breeze on a hot day, filling my lungs as I breathed her in. When she pulled back and blinked up at me, I felt the moment the Primordials slithered into me, stroking the inner corners of my body. Fallon grinned, lifting her hand to touch beneath my eyes. I knew my eyes probably glowed with the same gold that had consumed hers, the haze of arousal washing over me as I slid a hand beneath the curtain of her hair.

"Sunfire," I murmured, using my hold on her jaw to tip her head up once more and capture her mouth with mine more fully. She was pliant in my arms, none of the fight that I'd come to associate with her present as she molded her body to mine. She fit me like she belonged there, nestling into the swells and valleys of my body with hers. She reached between us, taking my cock in her hand and drawing a growl from me that shattered the last vestiges of my control.

Too rough, I thought distantly, warning the greedy, hungry voice that wasn't entirely my own. We may have shared the same desire, but I winced as my hands grasped Fallon by the waist and lifted her out of the water. I tossed her to the edge of the pool, cursing myself as she landed hard atop the edge. Instead of a grimace of pain, her face twisted into a bold grin and laughter bubbled up her throat.

I stared at her, waiting for her to show signs of pain and barely restraining the part of me that wanted nothing more than to go to her, to spread her wide and plunge inside so harshly that she would feel the imprint of me the next day.

Fallon worried her bottom lip with her teeth, leaning back on one hand and crooking me forward with a finger of her other. She spread her legs wide, hooking her feet along the edge of the bath and baring herself to my view. There was no insecurity in the movement, and I wondered briefly if that was a consequence of the Primordials riding her body and taking pleasure through her, or merely Fallon's confidence in her own body.

I hoped that confidence never went away, the woman who knew the spell she could weave over me with her beauty and her body.

I closed the distance quickly, far quicker than I should have been able to move, stepping into the gap she'd created between her legs. I claimed her mouth with mine, plunging my tongue inside the way I would my cock soon enough. She wrapped those long legs around me, pulling me tighter. So tight that my cock pressed against the seam of her, the heat of her core surrounding me and drawing a moan from me. I reached between us, desperate to guide myself inside, to feel her wrapped around me in truth.

She tore her mouth from mine, shaking her head mischievously. "If you want to fuck me, then you'd best prove you're worthy of my throne and my body first," she said, running a delicate hand through my deep auburn hair. She smiled as she pulled it, tugging me smoothly down her body.

I smiled against the skin of her breast, cupping her in one hand and tormenting her other nipple with my tongue. Her moan of satisfaction reached my ears, driving the other beings within me to growl in time with me. The sound reverberated off the trees as I slid my free hand between her thighs, covering it in her wet heat as I slid a finger into her and bit down on her breast. She pushed at my shoulders, knowing exactly what she wanted from me and *where* she wanted me, drawing twisted laughter from me as I lifted her legs onto my shoulders and slid my tongue through her. Tormentingly slow, I avoided the bundle of nerves as she writhed her hips, seeking release.

"Fucking asshole," she grumbled, tugging on the strands of hair at the top of my head. With startling force, she used that brutal grip to guide me to her clit, sighing happily when I finally smiled into her and gave her what she wanted. I worked her with my tongue, burying two fingers into her tight heat to stretch her open to take me. She shook beneath me, her body going taut as I explored every inch of her pussy, curling my fingers to stroke the spot inside her that made her eyes roll back in her head.

I smiled as I pulled my fingers out, straightening my body and earning a startled glare from Fallon. She'd been right on that edge, her pussy clamping down on me as she prepared for release. "You come on my cock," I said, guiding it to her entrance. She didn't push me away this time, arching her back so that she could stare down at the place where we joined. I slapped her clit with my head twice, watching as her oversensitive body jolted in response to the contact.

I glided myself lower, notching it against her as she wrapped her legs around my waist once more, and I drove inside. She was too tight, but so fucking wet that I slid through tender tissue, pulling back and then gliding forward again every time I met resistance.

"Fuck," she mumbled, dropping onto her back on the edge of the bath. Her hair spread over the grass, looking like part of the sacred nature of this place if it hadn't been for the way her face twisted in pleasure.

I drove deep, striking the end of her and filling her in the way I'd wanted since I laid eyes on her, unable to control myself. The haze of Primordial magic meant I was rougher than I should have been, taking her in deep, hard thrusts that made her gasp with each one. I couldn't wait to do it with that strange golden stare gone from her eyes, to look into her natural hazel hue and fuck her and her alone, without the Primordials within us.

I pulled back, snapping my hips forward to drive into her once more. She moaned, her back scraping along the ledge of the bath as she moved with the force of my thrusts. I took her hands in mine, threading our fingers together and pinning hers to the grass beneath her, stilling her body to the best of my ability. I made her hold her position as I picked up my pace, driving in and out of her with sharp, fast thrusts that spoke to the desperation I felt. I needed to fill her, needed to fuck her until she couldn't remember her own name.

I wanted to erase the separation between us, to mold our bodies into one, and she held her stare with mine as I used her body to do it.

"Harder," she whispered, her gasps ragged and torn as they came with each plunge of me within her. I gave her what she wanted, guiding one of her hands to her clit and using the combination of our fingers to work it. She tossed her head back, her breathing coming heavy and her cries growing louder. She whimpered as I took what I wanted, her own body seeking its pleasure from it.

"That's it. Fucking come for me," I murmured. Her mouth dropped open into a scream as she came, her pussy clamping down on me so tightly I couldn't help but follow her over the edge, spilling myself inside her. I stilled as I finished, leaving my cock inside her as I lifted her from the edge and pulled her down into the water with me. She wrapped her legs around me to aid in my support in spite of her exhaustion, resting her head on my shoulder as she fought to catch her breath.

I still felt the weight of the Primordials between us, the heat of their attention in my skin. Though they'd given us a brief reprieve, I knew they weren't yet done with us.

"Are you good?" I asked, taking advantage of the opportunity to speak without fearing the answer would come from the Primordials more than her.

Fallon raised her head, meeting my stare as a swirl of gold and hazel mixed in her eyes. She smiled, nodding tiredly as she leaned forward and kissed me tenderly.

It was a tenderness that came with hope attached, with the possibility for a future we could carve out together. We might not have been the couple people were expecting, but we could have affection between us without a mate bond.

We could have the love that came from choice, rather than destiny. She was the woman I'd chosen, not the one the Fates had determined was mine.

There was power in that.

We would find a way to do it together, united as King and Queen, husband and wife.

Twenty-Three

FALLON

Etan's ass hung off one of the steps, his feet planted a few steps lower and his legs spread slightly. Water sloshed around us as I rode him, moving to match his frenzied pace as he thrust up and into me. His brown eyes were even warmer than normal, ringed by gold as the Primordials used us to satiate their lust.

His mouth found my nipple, tongue circling the tender and swollen flesh as he worked it over. I felt my exhaustion in every muscle, in every place where our bodies came together over and over again without reprieve. Every time I thought Etan's cock couldn't continue to give, I found him hard and ready, seeking the heat between my thighs as soon as I caught my breath.

"Etan," I gasped, another orgasm threatening to consume me. It had long since become too much, my body so oversensitive that I couldn't really tell where one orgasm ended or the next began. My thighs quaked as I pressed my hands into Etan's chest, not caring what the pressure might have done to his back where he lay uncomfortably splayed over the steps. Rolling my hips over him and lost to the movements that were somehow both mine and not, I rubbed my clit against his body as he bucked his hips and dragged his cock through my swollen flesh.

As my orgasm crested, his fingers tightened on my ass, bruising in intensity as he too was lost to the magic of the sanctuary. My eyes closed as I tossed my head back in pleasure. His cock seemed to swell within me, growing even harder in the absence of his own orgasm—when mine usually dragged him over the edge with me.

A warm, balmy breeze blew through the clearing, bringing with it the scent of summer in a rush of sand and salt. My eyes opened slowly, finding Etan staring up at me in awe as the breeze caught my hair and blew it back from my face. Bright orange and coral petals from the nearby dahlia plants spread with the wind. They swirled around us like a cyclone, surrounding me as the wind picked up stronger.

Reality crept back in, chasing away some of the magic that made my hips continue to move in spite of the summer storm surging around us. The branches of the trees creaked as they angled in the wind, but Etan released my ass to grab my hands in his and draw my attention back to him.

"With me, Sunfire. Don't you dare fucking stop," he said, thrusting up so sharply that a pinch of pain speared through me as he struck the end of me. He adjusted his position, releasing only my right hand to sit and using his hand to support his weight so that he brought us face-to-face. His mouth came down on mine all over again, his tongue surging into my mouth and stoking the flames of desire all over again.

The breeze kissed my breasts, the warmth of it gliding down the valley between them and over my stomach, teasing the place where Etan and I were joined. I gasped into his mouth, pulling back at the unfamiliar feeling.

"What—" I started to ask, but Etan shook his head and guided my hand to his shoulder. Once I gripped him, he moved his hand back to my ass and guided me up and down, moving me on his cock.

"Don't stop. Let the magic take what it needs," he said, his voice gentle and reassuring even though I knew he *had* to feel it. Soft, teasing touches of the wind explored us as we moved, barely a tickle like a feather, but present no less. It surrounded us, wrapping us in an embrace as Etan groaned beneath me.

His brow furrowed as he crashed his mouth onto mine, this orgasm that came barreling toward us feeling different from all the rest. I tossed my head back as I rolled my hips, bringing both of us closer to it. His mouth sealed over my nipple, teeth gently pinching the flesh and tongue working it over as I stared up at the sky.

The sun seemed to brighten as I watched, my body heating from within. Suddenly too warm, I wished Etan and I had been farther into the water so it could cool my skin.

He shoved his hand between us, brushing two fingers over my clit twice before I shattered, shaking as the orgasm consumed me. I was vaguely aware of his groan that matched my cry, his warmth filling me to the brim.

I hadn't even caught my breath in the aftershocks of pleasure when the sun flashed, the brightness of it blinding me as I closed my eyes to protect them. All-consuming pain spread through me, barreling down my throat and burning me from the inside out. The side of my neck felt like I'd been burned alive, the fire trailing down my arm. I peeked out from sunblind eyes to stare at the once black Fae Marks as they bled into red.

I knew the moment Imelda's wards failed within me, the magic of the Summer Court filling me in a way it had never done before. This was different, this was *more*, and Etan retracted his hands from my skin with a gasp as if I'd burned him.

"Sunfire," he said, his voice gentle. I tried to stand, releasing his cock from my body, only to find that the parts of me that were within the water could not move. Locked together, I had to hope that the fire would not consume him, too. He risked the burn to cup my face in his hands, seemingly unbothered when light pulsed off my skin and crept along his forearms. "You're okay. It's just Rheaghan's magic, the magic of the Summer Court, choosing its new host. Stop fighting it."

"It was supposed to choose you. I'm just your Queen," I snapped, my teeth gritted together to fight the pain.

Etan smiled softly, touching his mouth to mine so gently it felt like he hugged my heart itself. "It was never going to be me, *min solios*," he said, offering me his term of endearment in the old tongue.

My sun.

I drew in a deep breath, grimacing when the summer air around us poured itself down my throat, sinking into me in a way that made it feel as if I would never be cold again. My skin seemed to reflect the light of sunshine, shimmering lightly as I settled and accepted the magic that would not leave me be.

Accepted it as mine.

I sighed, the pain fading as soon as the magic had taken root within me. I shoved it down deep to the place where I could feel the incredibly faint remnants of what had been Imelda's wards, their edges frayed and burned. But it clung to the wisps of them that remained, as if Rheaghan's magic had simply strode through a door she left open.

I would not become a monster. I would not become like the woman who had made me.

Etan stood with me in his arms, bringing me deeper into the water and allowing it to cool my overheated skin. The gold was gone from his eyes now, leaving only Etan as the Primordials of this place fled, fed and satiated from all we'd given.

But that did not stop his cock from stirring all over again. Where we had previously been frenzied and passionate, seeking pleasure in each other's bodies, we now moved in slow glides as he pressed my back against the edge of the pool and spread me wide.

Before, our passion had been for *them*.

This one was for *us*.

Twenty-Four

ETAN

Fallon was quiet as she caught her breath, her face tucked into the crook of my neck. I had no desire to leave her, but also didn't want to crush her with my weight unnecessarily. Every one of my limbs trembled, not from exertion but the crash of adrenaline as the last dredges of magic fled.

The choice had been made, and while I'd long suspected that Fallon would be the one who was chosen as the true heir, it didn't ease the tiny sting I felt. It meant she *had* to have magic of her own, that it was the Summer Court she truly called home, and even when she'd started to open up to me, that was one secret she'd kept for herself.

The Summer Court wouldn't have chosen her to lead otherwise.

Fallon sighed and stood, sliding herself out from beneath me with a shaky smile. She seemed suddenly uncomfortable in her nudity, a flush hitting her cheeks when my gaze lingered on the curve of her breast before gliding up to her breathtakingly ethereal face. She looked at home in this place—this sanctuary that was filled with mysticism and where magic coated the very air. She couldn't seem to meet my gaze, her attention pointedly elsewhere.

I followed after her as she found her underwear on the bank beside the pool, tugging it up her legs and hiding that part of her from my view.

"Talk to me, *min solios*," I said, touching a hand to her shoulder. She spun to face away from me with an odd expression, but didn't move away from the contact altogether. She shook her head as if she couldn't get a handle on her thoughts.

"I don't know how," she admitted, her voice trembling.

"How to what?" I asked, pulling her closer. She didn't seem to mind my nudity or the way I touched her, my arms wrapping around her waist. She turned and circled her arms around me as if she craved that closeness, returning the embrace in a way that communicated it wasn't her body that was revolting against what had happened. She buried her face in my chest, taking deep breaths that worried me.

"How to anything! It was stressful enough thinking I was just going to be your queen, but I was willing to do it if it meant I could have some power to choose for myself. I didn't expect the magic to choose me. What does that even mean for us? For my freedom?" she asked, the urgency in her voice conveying just how panicked she was by the thought.

"Nothing needs to be any different than it would have been if the magic had chosen me as its host, Fallon. I will still be King and you will still be Queen, and we will still work together to rule our court to the best of our ability," I said, hoping the words would reassure her.

"Yeah?" she asked, her voice shaking. "Then tell me this, what if one of us were to find a mate? Who would remain as the ruler then?"

I gritted my teeth, hating the answer. Fallon didn't want to rule in truth, not yet anyway, and the Summer Court had been my haven from the world for as long as I could remember. But the answer was sure and swift; the magic had left no room for doubt.

"You do," I said, the very mention of her mate enough to make my blood feel like fire in my veins. I'd always had a strong reaction to the notion of losing Fallon to another male, but it felt different now that I'd had her.

Now that I knew how she felt wrapped around me, and I never wanted to leave that embrace.

I hated to think it, but on the off chance that Fallon had a Fae mate and not a human one, the monochromatic color of her Fae Marks meant that he would be a Summer Court Fae. It almost made me not want to take her home, not want to risk losing the chemistry we had found together.

"I'm not ready for this," she said, her voice filled with the sting of tears.

"I don't understand. You were willing when you stepped into the pool. What happened?" I asked, trying to catch her gaze as I pulled back. But Fallon studiously avoided me, turning her head to the side in a way that broke something inside of me.

The need for distance didn't make sense. None of this did.

"It was supposed to be just sex, Etan," she said, her voice soft with the traces of emotion she didn't want to convey. She was pushing me away and I knew it, and I knew that meant I'd gotten too close. She couldn't dismiss what had happened as an effect of the magic because she'd allowed me to make love to her even without it.

It was supposed to be.

The words struck me in the chest, the casual admission in them making me tuck her loose wet hair behind her ear. "I've had plenty of *just sex* and that is not what that was. For either of us," I said to reassure her that she wasn't alone in those feelings. I hadn't expected it to be so much more than what I'd experienced before, but somehow it was everything.

"I will not be owned," she asserted, but she didn't move away from the affection of my touch. The words didn't make sense in the context of the conversation, especially not when I hadn't made any mention of attempting to own her.

"I don't have any interest in owning you, *min solios*," I said, snagging Fallon by the chin. I turned her to look at me, my heart racing as her stare dropped to my chest. "Why won't you look at me?"

Her eyes shuddered closed, her breathing coming in harsh pants and her heart beating out of her chest. When she finally tipped her head up and thrust her eyes open, sunfire flashed through them in a sudden spark. I felt it all the way down to my toes, molten heat tearing through me and centering on my *viniculum*, where it pulsed with deeper red.

My eyes widened as I stared at Fallon, understanding what she had felt before I did. The bond that the offering had revealed pulsed between us, an invisible thread that could never be severed. The woman I'd thought I'd chosen for myself in the absence of fate was no longer.

Because Fallon was my mate.

> Fallon and Etan's story will continue, along with Caldris and Estrella's, in book five of the Of Flesh & Bone series, *What Roams Beneath the Stars*.

Acknowledgments

I can hardly believe the journey my love of writing has taken me on. If you'd told me when I was a child that one day, I'd be writing the acknowledgments for my thirty-fourth book, I never would have believed it. It seems impossible and far-fetched, but that is what *The Heir & the Spare* is for me.

There are so many people I have to thank for supporting me through my unorthodox career, people who have always believed in me. My family and friends are my rock, and as much as they distract me from this job at every turn they possibly can, they refill my cup with so much love and inspire me every day.

To my readers, whose love for my words and my stories has kept me going through some of my darkest moments. This career can be incredibly isolating, but knowing you're out there waiting for more books makes me feel less alone.

To my daughter, for always being unapologetically herself. One day, you'll be a strong, independent woman who takes the world by storm, and it is my privilege to give you the space to bloom. Thank you for the daily reminder of quiet perseverance and determination.

To my son, for showing kindness to everyone you meet without fail. Your gentle care and empathy for others always gives me hope for a better tomorrow. Thank you for being the hope that keeps me going—even when the world gets dark.

To my friends, you know who you are. The constant companions who talk me off the cliff when I'm being dramatic, or the ones who encourage me to stop people-pleasing my way through life. Thank you for seeing *me* first always, and lending your ear and support when I'm in a low.

And lastly, and perhaps a bit unexpectedly, thank you to the ones who *didn't* believe in me. Thank you to the ones who filled me with petty spite, because they told me I would never succeed in this career, and the ones who actively wished I'd fail. You were maybe my greatest motivation, because proving you wrong has been one of my greatest achievements in life.

ABOUT THE AUTHOR

Harper L. Woods is the *New York Times*—and *USA Today*—bestselling fantasy romance alter ego for Adelaide Forrest. Raised in small-town Vermont, her passion for reading was born during long winters spent with her face buried between the pages of a book. She began to pass the time by writing short stories that quickly turned into full-length fiction. Since that time, she has published more than thirty books and has plans for many more. When she isn't writing, Woods can be found spending time with her two young kids, curling up with her dog, dreaming about travel to distant lands, or designing book covers she'll never have enough time to use.